Ca

THE LAST LOOK

V

VINTAGE

Published by Vintage 1999

2 4 6 8 10 9 7 5 3 1

Copyright © Candida Clark 1998

First published in Great Britain by
Chatto & Windus in 1998

Vintage
Random House, 20 Vauxhall Bridge Road,
London SW1V 2SA

Random House Australia (Pty) Limited
20 Alfred Street, Milsons Point, Sydney
New South Wales 2061, Australia

Random House New Zealand Limited
18 Poland Road, Glenfield, Auckland 10,
New Zealand

Random House South Africa (Pty) Limited
Endulini, 5A Jubilee Road, Parktown 2193,
South Africa

Random House UK Limited Reg. No. 954009

A CIP catalogue record for this book
is available from the British Library

ISBN 0 09 927256 3

Printed and bound in Norway by
AIT Trondheim AS, 1999

For Tim

With many thanks to Jonny Geller, Rebecca Carter, Jonathan Burnham and Kate Burvill. And, of course, to Cassandra Clark, Alan Sharpe and Saskia Howard.

Anna Sergeyevna, too, came in. She sat down in the third row, and when Gurov looked at her his heart contracted, and he understood clearly that for him there was in the whole world no creature so near, so precious, and important to him.

From Chekhov's *The Lady with the Dog*

It's always the same, so what d'you think you're going to do about it? Damn trees, drains, roads, tomato plants, soil, heat, kids and women is more or less what I was saying or maybe thinking when I first saw her walking towards me down the long driveway at the end of that hot day in June when the poplars swayed in the soft wind from off the sea, the birds were going crazy in the last slow ebb of dusk and every damn thing about the place contrived to try to make me think how lucky I was, how life was sweet and that I should just shut up with my miserable thoughts and get on with it.

So I was swearing and stamping around, pulling up tomato plants, cutting up my hands until they were red raw, nearly bleeding, scowling at the blue sky without a single cloud to blame, feeling the full weight of my rotten life around my neck, choked up by the unmitigated doom of it all, then there she was, smiling and laughing with that Swiss guy who brought her to see me without a clue about what would happen between us. Seeing me, red-faced and foul-mouthed, or foul-thoughted, I forget which, she smiled, and said, 'You need a hand?' And from that moment, if not a few seconds earlier, from the instant when I first saw her, before she saw me, everything changed and my life was over.

The sorry thing was, I never realised how lucky I was *before* I met her until I met her. From then on I was cursed. I swear to God, that woman put a hex on me. And there wasn't a single damn thing I could do about it.

You'll forget all about me soon enough bothered me. It was so unfair and I knew it wasn't true. Years later, when other men in other lives elicited protests from me in a similar manner – 'You'll soon forget about me.' 'Don't be silly, how could I?' – I'd smile to myself, enjoying the lie. Now I think about how the trees appeared to weep that morning when I left. I am walking barefoot across the stony grass towards the house, unable to think of anything else but my skin and how it has changed. Before, it was the dividing line between me and the world, now it offers no protection and I am exposed to every colour, smell and touch, which flood through me, familiarising me with the odour of death, so that I tremble with a strange discomfort. It is all his fault. He has made me watchful, restless and alert, approaching everything with senses bared, vulnerable to shocks.

He isn't there when I go into the kitchen, so I creep upstairs to his bedroom, hoping he'll be there but also hoping I can have just one minute in his room without him, to see how that feels. The bare wooden stairs creak slightly with my weight as I

3

pad up to the top corridor, remembering the walls and windows by feel. Last night it was dark and moonlit. Everything was done by touch. Flesh and stubborn concrete, grating my back as I pulled him towards me in a desperate, wrestling embrace. Now I can see and so I'm staring hard at every detail of the place where he lives: the pale-blue, woman-chosen carpet running down the middle of the corridor, the dirty yellow blinds pulled up above the windows which look out on to the pool and the other side of the house, three doors, the third his bedroom, the second the bathroom, the first a mildew-smelling store-room, stacked high with discarded papers.

In the bathroom I sniff the things he uses on his body, running my tongue along the handle of his heavy ivory razor, feeling its brief weight in the palm of my hand, then lightly, against my fingers. I smile when I inhale the unfamiliar scents, unused, more woman-chosen things, lined up like protests along the top of the bathroom cupboard. I look at the signs of half-hearted vanity, the vitamins and whimsically chosen creams. I find evidence of familiar use in few things here: a strange-looking oil with a sharply evaporating smell for shaving, a rough mitten for the shower, a long, dark grey towelling robe, an efficient-looking pair of scissors. On the wall, there is a tall, vertically hanging mirror and I think of his beautiful nakedness shining from it daily and feel suddenly resentful, staring back at my lone reflection, hating the world and my age, full of loathing for my brash young body, out of step with who I have become. I close the door to the bathroom gently, trying to work out how he closes it, walking carefully to see if I can feel his footsteps on the blue carpet, looking for prints, finding none.

Along the corridor the slanting early morning sunlight already burns through the window-panes, heating the dust-steady air. There is a look of cheerfulness about this house. Something impersonal and temporary which suggests a lack of interest in its decoration. The door to his bedroom stands open so that the room is filled with light from the window opposite. The whole house is silent, but I hesitate for a moment on the threshold of this private room, unable to fathom the image of my shape intertwined with his on the bed. I realise that that is how I will always remember him most clearly: in darkness. Close up, close enough for me to feel the hairs on his body rubbed beneath my fingertips, roughened beneath my searching tongue, his skin-smell deep within my breath, hot and damp like a raw thing in birth. But it is bright, gloriously bright now, and the room is made new by the sunlight. I wonder with what casualness I could turn to him, were he to come up the stairs right now, and say, 'So can I stay? Can I? It's really very simple.' Laughing, perhaps, to give him a way out, hating him if he found it too quickly. But I don't want him to come up the stairs now because I am already over-full with him. I have walked into the space he's left behind in this room and I can feel him all around me like an embrace.

When I lie down on the bed I think I can find the warmth of his body, but perhaps it is just the heat of the sun. So I stretch out, corpse-like, on the mattress, folding my hands across my chest, and stay still for a moment, breathing, storing it all up, feeling unbelievably calm. Only the surface of me is mad panicked by the thought of leaving which will be soon, almost now. But I lie there for a moment longer, discovering cracks in the old paintwork on the ceiling, tracing their odd lightning-strikes across the roof of my sight for a second longer before getting up and tiptoeing out of the room, glancing back over my shoulder as I leave, unsuperstitious, just wanting one last look before I go.

And there is still no one in the house when I go downstairs, watchful, knowing I might be found out. *But I've done nothing.* There is the smell of coffee, though, and I realise that in the time when I was upstairs someone came into the kitchen. But it's not him. It's the Swissman, fretting about his luggage, the drive back to New York, shooting me a look of distaste when he sees me coming down the stairs, suspecting too much, then baffled when *he* breezes in from outside. He ignores me for a few seconds of over-solicitous attention for the Swissman, before turning to me to smile in that particular way he has, tilting his snowy-haired head slightly sideways, his pale grey eyes glinting wonderfully, like the flash of a storm glimpsed over the horizon at sea. His smile matters to me, I think, despairing, wondering if he can guess – how could he? – what I've been doing upstairs. I feel guilty like a thief. I have something secret now that I didn't take away when I crept downstairs before dawn, slipping back through the night to my own room on the far side of the house.

~

The tomato plants were good that year, that was one thing she couldn't take away from me. The ripe fruit nearly fell off into your hands, which was one of the reasons I was so angry that day she arrived. Some kids from across the way had stolen a whole load of them. I swear I saw the little monsters prancing around in the bushes later on, their evil, grinning faces dripping savagely with the blood-red juice. So she wasn't about to go and get impressed by my tomato plants, which was an irritation to me from the start. After all, they could have been prize-winning plants, if I'd ever bothered to take them to a competition. And the truth is that until then they'd given me such pleasure I could go down to the patch and gawp at them for hours, just sit there like an idiot staring at them, telling myself that at least that was something, at least this year the tomatoes were good, whatever else might go wrong. But the girl changed all that and I decided to let them go to seed anyhow, just like the rest of my life. It seemed appropriate that way. I mean, why hang on to one sorry aspect when it's easier to let it go the way of all things, die a natural death? So the tomatoes had to go and by the end of the season I vowed there'd be nothing left of them but the pile of cow-shit I'd used as fertiliser the year before when they were good. Prize winners, I swear. Shit is good for them.

There are birds, dark-winged in the tree-tops, and a blue sky serene overhead, high above the breeze from off the hidden sea. He is talking to the Swissman, standing a few yards away from me on the white veranda which runs around the house. Seeing him now, like this, I know I've been blessed with meeting him. He is my twin and this thought makes me glad, even though it is impossible, all of it, with no hope of a future, just the present moments, just one weekend.

'You have your whole life ahead of you,' he said, sadly caressing my hair as we lay together on the bed last night, delirious with moonlight. *Yes I have,* I thought with equal sadness but hope, too, which made all the difference, thinking in secret *And what a life I can make it now. I'll wait for no one. I'll race through time, hot-time waiting for no one, no need to wait because I've had you and you're my twin and once you're dead there'll be no one left for me, not one solitary soul alive who could even potentially be you and I'm glad about that beyond belief, you have no idea how glad I am about that,* saying, 'Don't say that, it makes me miserable. What will I do without you?' Thinking *Everything*. All those alone moments ahead of me somehow marvellous-seeming because there'd be no space left alongside them for regret, because regret has now, by meeting him, become something impossible. *I will never have to wait for love because here it is and I've given everything to it.* I smile to myself as I think this, feeling his dear sweet body entering mine, filling me up with himself, breathing his last into me like a desperate absolution before death, but absolution at a price: the burden of his life. Realising this, I hate him for it, though I'm grateful, too, because it merely confirms what I know myself to be. And now I can be alone, at last, no one can disturb me with false promises of happiness because it's happened, sooner than I'd dared hope for, and sooner still it will be gone and then I can be alone until I die, with this dead weight of albatross love around my neck.

I close my eyes briefly to the brightness of the morning, remembering: his body pressed against me, hot-breath words muttered against my ear as he told me, 'They say I haven't long to live, but you know I don't mind at all.' I looked hard at his face then, pulling him closer towards me, watching for the lie in his eyes, seeing no sign of it yet, but suspecting it soon and afraid for him, terrified for the moment when he would see his mistake. 'I have no regrets about my life is why,' he said, 'and nor should you,' his eyes throwing the challenge at my feet. 'Because everything is material for work, don't ever forget that. However deep something cuts, it is of no consequence whatsoever unless you take a hold of it and use it, turn it around so it can't cause you any more anguish than is absolutely necessary for that simple act of creation. You see,' he said, looking away from me then, 'work is the only thing that matters. Everything else is worthless in comparison and that's the truth.'

I kissed him when he said that and believed him, too, even though I wondered at what moment and for what reason he'd given up trusting in this himself because I could tell he had, even though he still suspects it to be true, thinking: *So that's how I will live, just as he did.* The ritual eating up, digestion and meticulous vomit of even the most precious circumstance, all things become vital for living, though nothing, in fact, of any importance whatsoever, other than as fuel for writing. I should be glad, not sorry, that he's shown me the best way and so early in my life. And besides, I'd suspected as much already and this is merely confirmation because why else would it have happened? Why else? If I was meant to find some lasting dream of happiness then everything would have happened differently. The brute reality of our circumstance, his imminent death, my being married, become insignificant obstacles in comparison with the truth I am facing up to about life and the whole set-up which is simple, more straightforward than I'd anticipated: everyone is alone. And everything else merely follows on in abject certainty from this unambiguous premise. So being alone means that every second which warmly rushes along the surface of life, those moments with other people, are nothing more than glimpses of other lives which could equally well have been your own and anyway are of equal insignificance, however wildly they might burn inside you. The job of those who feel this: to remind others, remark to them that they are in fact alive and alone, this minuscule nudge and observation through words being infinitely more important than any chance of happiness, which anyway, I realise now, is a lie, at least for me. So that since there is no chance *then there is no chance*, though in some other, truer life, I am seeing the world with his eyes, the horror of loneliness suspended softly above me with this new, shared look upon the world.

Empty-handed, I am left on the outside, wondering only how long can it last? Suspecting: for ever. Feeling the ecstatic free-fall into this true vision, with everything flooding through me like a wild, cool blessing, freezing up my heart into this state of impeccable memory but memory with eyes. Glad beyond belief that I have seen the contradiction so soon: the treacherous vision of becoming un-alone, but still this shared vision of imposs-ibility mattering more than anything else and being the only thing worth fighting for, though from now on I will be fighting with a ghost because even now I'm on the brink of leaving for ever, more sure of this madness at the heart of things than of anything else. But then, I'm only as sure of this as I am of the impression of him upon my body, so that still I can feel his hands upon me, the imprint of his fists against my flesh something undeniably certain but already from a different time and place, already nothing more than myth. And if this isn't the way my life should be, I tell myself, then why else would I have met him now and in this circum-stance, utterly without hope?

All this flashes past my mind as I stand in the shadow of the building, ready to go. But of course I am reluctant to leave and so I wait, thinking of other endings. There are none. I turn my back on the house and think how simple my life will be now that this weekend is over. Emphatically not the start of something risky and unsettling. Merely an ending, an efficient way of paring down the diameters of my life, which must be a good thing.

He looks back at me as I stand hesitating in the doorway and I see his face and white unruly hair bathed in morning sunlight, suddenly making him appear beatific and remote, almost like an angel. I can't help but feel submerged anger at his life, loving and jealous of his past all at once, almost wishing I'd bitten into his flesh last night so hard that I'd scar him for ever. He beckons to me with a lift of his chin and I go towards him, trying to hold his gaze, but he's looked away on some excuse too soon so I just stand beside him and the Swissman, suddenly feeling that quick familiar joy at the proximity of his body that I can't explain. My mind races past images of me and him at parties, in bars, in the street, in dark theatres, merely sliding along through life beside one another, living in similar spaces and finding happiness easier and greater that way, that's all. But I don't linger on these images, I tear past them, burning them up as I go along, watching the ashes float off into the implacable blue.

He swings my bag over his shoulder and lifts it easily into the car, staring hard and angry at it as it sits there, stowed away. I get in, close the door and wind down the window, watching him intently, being sure to record the tricksy time-worn details that will slip from memory. The pollen is high and when I sneeze he whips off the red kerchief from round his neck and gives it to me, so fast it's as though he was just waiting for me to do it. I'm glad for his anticipation, inhaling deeply the scent of his skin and sweat from the fresh cotton, trying not to breathe any other air but that, almost losing a grip and tipping myself out of the car on to the ground to thrash around in the stony mud and wail against the stupid unfairness of it all. But of course I don't do this. Instead I smile and thank him as the car engine spits and groans, and I put on my sun-glasses so he realises that I don't want him to see me crying.

As we begin to curve out of the drive his lone figure is abject, resolute, stubborn and proud, suspicious of death. Without him, I realise, I have my strong self back again and I'm appalled at my strength. *What is it good for now?* It's just a reminder of my loneliness. *And that's the truth*, I tell myself. I feel safe and lost and pointless. I watch him in the rear-view mirror and pull the lid over my life, hating everything but him, knowing at that moment that I'll never want anyone else's body inside mine, arms around me, nor sight to share as we gaze wildly at the moon on a pale summer's evening with no sound around

us but our out-breaths mingling with the restless
breeze.

~

I was watching her closely from the first moment she arrived. I knew I had to keep my eye on her. I knew it'd be easy to catch her out with just one look she'd let slip across her face, slippity slip, sliding past, unnoticed by everyone but me, then I'd have her and everything would be fine again and I could get back to normal. So I watched her closely, knowing that I'd see it soon enough. I waited and watched, but she wasn't letting on. I could have kicked myself for all the times I took my eyes off her. Those would have been the moments when I'd have seen it on her face, the instants when I looked away, it had to be then, didn't it? Because I watched her like a hungry hawk the rest of the time and she didn't show it, not once.

I've been through each second of her being here a thousand thousand times if I've been through it at all and at no point did she show what I just knew she was thinking about me: *Sorry fool, with nothing but memories and tomato plants*. She would have been right as well, which is my point.

She walked towards me up the drive, laughing

and smiling with that Swiss guy, and as soon as I saw them together I realised he hadn't the first idea about who she was, or *what* she was in her heart. I wondered, at first, if he was screwing her. But the more I looked at her small, slender body and thought about his gangly limbs wrapped around it, the more I thought about her long red hair tangled up in his dry, spidery fingers, the more absurd it seemed, so I tried not to think about it, it disgusted me too much.

So there she was, walking up my driveway and my first thought was *Oh hell, not now. Not now I'm happy and alone.* I hadn't expected her to be at all lovely. From the way he'd described her I'd anticipated some dull, aloof bitch whom I'd merely tolerate, counting the seconds until she left. But it was her, so I had to think fast.

She looked at me strangely as she watched me hug the Swissman, which should have been some kind of clue or hope for me, but of course I didn't see it. I took her bag and carried it over to the house. First I showed him to the place where he'd sleep, then I showed her. I had real difficulty taking her to her room, the bed being this big, obvious piece of furniture in the middle of the floor, making it seem instantly unnatural for us not to fall upon it, upon each other, and feast on the shock of meeting like this. At least, that's how it felt.

Some days I sit in the chair where I sat when she arrived, looking at the space where she was on the sofa, the place where she sat, drinking the vodka I'd given her, looking kind of nervous, a bit uncomfortable in her smart city clothes. But I liked that, her edginess in that dressy thing she was wearing, and I could see that beneath the jacket, beneath the dress, she was naked and I had to look away, pay too much attention to the Swissman, resenting him for occupying my sight when all the while it was her I wanted to be looking at, no one else.

So that's it. No going back or forwards. The racing engine tearing us through the afternoon is no more than an illusion of movement. Really, I'm pinned to this abject, brief moment of leaving, caught insect-like and ridiculous. *Impossible* smashes me in the soft parts of my mind each time I take a look round the corners of hope, so I give up looking pretty soon.

The road soothes me. It matches my new vision of the world: a flattened-out landscape. Everything wildly bright with meaning. Everything meaning nothing whatsoever. All things become harmonious with hot discord, touching me with equal violence and tenderness, filling me up with desperate conviction and leaving me empty, overflowing with disbelief. I've become disengaged from the world to the point of being shaken to my core by everything. Like an unravelling vein, the road draws me along itself disgustingly. There are trees swaying, flowers blooming, farmers harvesting, huge pale birds screaming wildly in the tree-tops. It's a beautiful day. Just look! There's a

21

lovely smell of gas, too, and the faintest whiff of burnt rubber as we keel around corners.

The Swissman is driving. He turns up the volume of his favourite track which I hate. He tells me, 'It's a sad situation, no, the way he is keeping himself alone? And they say he only has a few months left to live, maybe less,' sliding me a vicious, narrow-eyed look, eager to fuel his suspicion. 'But I thought it would be interesting for you to meet him and, anyway, I wanted to see him one last time,' he says, a pathetic attempt to claim the weekend. My hands, I can't help them, edge nervously towards the door handle. I long to leap from the car and tumble like a rock across the verge and into one of the wonderful scorched fields, fire-blackened and fallow, or end up in a ditch to die there like a rat, still twitching as it falls discreetly into its unknown death. But I stay still and just stare ahead at the morning in front of me. I don't turn back.

My skin is sore and should be dripping with pus and bleeding even, scabrous and covered with welts where he grilled me with his kisses and gnashing teeth. On the inside I should be gravel-rough and difficult to touch. There should be unexpected holes where he punctured my flesh, boldering his way into me like a dumb fighter, but still, a fighter with soft hands. All I have, though, are a few bruises, mainly between my thighs where I clutched him hard to keep him trapped there until I was through, swollen lips that feel utterly unfamiliar as though beaten, once, briskly, with a lump of weird pig-iron, and nipples that are red raw beneath the silk of my dress, idiotic reminders of something that barely happened.

Gleaming. The road is gleaming, a shimmer of asphalt intention spinning itself out in front of me as I stare it down, appalled by its consistency. When the midday sun hits it, wham, directly over-head, I find something deeply satisfying about the whiplash lines down the central reservation, whacking into the road, on and on, shooting out from beneath me as I sit dead still in the passenger seat, not paying any attention to the day beyond the minute staring details I can't avoid, which fill my head up with facts about the world that mean nothing absolutely.

I try to get in my mind's eye an image of how the road would look were I lying beneath the axle of the car, face-down and staring, my nose centi-metres from the glassy surface. The image makes me nauseous and I have an overwhelming urge to curl up my toes, turning them back on themselves, away from the flying tarmac surface.

We pass gas stations, lone tenement farms, small towns, big towns, vast fields of over-ripe grass and bubbling corn, pile-ups and diners, tea-vans and parked trucks, trailers and signs to places I'll never go, with lunatic names, cows standing patiently in the fields, sheep jostling aimlessly, pigs shitting in their pens and wild-eyed chickens, evil to look at, all of this life and activity whirring past us as we drive along the road, now become silvery in the light of early afternoon.

I don't look back because that would be like grinning at the moon, pointless and hopeful for nothing. But the road! It is running through me, burning right through me like lightning straight into my brain's grey cushion of purpose, slicing it conveniently in two, showing me with perfect clarity the pattern of my life from now on. I watch my two lives peel apart, gaping open to reveal the monstrous separation between the life inside, the place where I really live and, miraculously, where he saw me, and the other life which I am returning to right now, the life which I never lived and will from now on live in even less than before. I feel the hot light of the silver road rip me down the middle so that my cunt heaves with emptiness, lurching sea-sickishly between my legs as the two halves of me fall open like an over-ripe lotus plant, cut with a deliberate knife. I cross my legs and sit on my hands so that I do not make a grab for my crotch to staunch the ache running from my cunt right through me in great torrents of electrifying grief. I catch sight of myself in the wing mirror and at the moment before recognition I realise that I half expected to see someone entirely changed, or at least for my insides to be turned out to reveal the grotesque fact of who I am, at last given licence. But I look fine. I don't look any different from before. I keep my beady eye on the road, watching the signs, merely making sense of the route we're taking back up to the city.

~

Night fell soon after they arrived, the darkly moonlit sky blackening the windows. You've got to keep things shut tight on nights like this. I have a mosquito problem, so I have to be vigilant, keep all the doors and windows closed or else the little shits come in and get busy on my skin in the dead of night. I'm susceptible. They can't seem to get enough of my juicy flesh.

I felt a bit short of breath like it was airless, so I tried to keep still as I talked, not rush around too much, but I couldn't help myself, it was impossible to sit motionless with her there on the couch a few feet away. She still had her jacket on but I could see the warm glow of her newly tanned skin as she bent forward to pick up her glass from the low table, her long russet-red hair glinting in the lamplight like a summer meadow on fire. I could see that she was restless. She kept pulling her jacket around her as if she was cold in a way to make it look like she wasn't all dressed up. But I liked that, her discomfort. It made me feel easier, more like I belonged here, she didn't. This is my home, after all.

I was curious to see what she would wear the next day.

She drank hard and fast. I like that in a woman. I mean, I don't normally like it at all but she seemed more at ease that way, revealing a weakness I could relate to, get hold of and mull over when she'd gone off to sleep. When it was time to turn in, me and the other guy, we both escorted her back over to her room, treating her real chivalrous, like she was royalty, but I was hard just thinking about her undressing and slipping beneath the cool cotton sheets, wondering if she wore anything at night, imagining that she didn't, she wasn't the type. So we did all that, the big show, men of the world, like I have young girls to stay every day of the week at my place. But all the time, while I was trying not to think about how hard I was just being in the same room as her, I was thinking fast about what I could do next, wishing the other guy wasn't there but glad beyond belief, glad in a way that almost made me panic to think about the contrary scenario, glad that he'd brought her here in the first place even if she did mess up my life for good after that.

The car I'm in joins the metal slug shifting along the edge of the island towards the bridge. The traffic, become slow-moving, seems watchful of the city with its spinning verticals, dreaming on upstaring into the celestial stinking blue, and I start to breathe less deeply, automatically adjusting to the pretty air-borne poisons. At the earliest opportunity, I lose the Swissman. 'I have to go shopping,' I say, and get him to let me out of the car.

Now that I am by myself I can try to pull the city back around me for protection. But the damage is done. I'm not alone any more. I have my eyes open and I feel everything with stripped-back skin, efficiently. There is no respite from the hot inrush of sensation, the bawling misfit voices feverish against my eardrums, the dead air's ooze around my throat. I am whipped raw in an instant by things which should be without significance. But when your imagination has been given licence to set fire to your mind every lunatic thing makes perfect sense. That's what he did for me, at least. And I'm still fizzing with the instant nostalgia it entails. I'm grateful, too, and each out-breath and thud of my heart is a prayer of thanks, making me glad to my guts for the way he speared me to the arrow of time while he remained intransigent, fixed on his own final death-trajectory, watching me politely from beneath the black cedars, upon his lips the smiling echo of that wishful declaration *You'll forget about me soon enough.*

The streets sweat, steam pouring from the vents in the hot tarmac like the breath of a wrinkle-backed hell-monster, grinding its muscles just below the surface of the city, struggling to get the vertical pikes, the skyscrapers, off its body. The more it struggles, the more the pikes stick deep. I want to get a hold of the streets and slow them down, soothe them for a moment, but it's no use and I'm like a flea making the city's skin scratchier the more I walk. But I must walk. Pacing out the grids becomes a dance of determined anger as I stomp and hesitate, stomp and hesitate, trying not to be sick at the sight of the implausible buildings, swaying like reeds in the light breeze from off the Atlantic, funnelling through the harbour to whip up a storm of flying paper and cursing animals at every street corner.

It is late afternoon now. High up above, the sunlight sets the building tops on fire with obscene brightness and at street level the grey monotony is appalling. No one looks up and in their eyes there are no questions, only defeat, or what comes before defeat: trepidation, that piss-stinking relic of terror.

I stop to contemplate all of this for the merest of moments, beneath the red-striped awning of a deli which is fragrant with pigmeat and hot cheese, but the pause makes me restless and I am overwhelmed by a sensation of physical illegitimacy but mental licence, the jumping dissonance of these sensations making me want to hum like a blind beggar, feeling eyes upon me in the dusky afternoon, surreptitious, rheumy eyes, like the investigative tentacles of an underwater creature with neat little fangs, sharp as knives. I hate to wait and I'm jealous as hell of people who loiter openly. I get moving again pretty quickly, nervous of the eyes and tentacles swarming around me in the darkening streets. I try to look at their faces, but everyone stares at the pavement or at some point in the diminishing vortex of streets behind me. I go faster and soon I'm swimming in the torrents of surface motion along the main arteries of the city, swimming with the current, faster and faster uptown, intently sperm-like with the flow of traffic.

In the gloom, from time to time, I think I see his face. Turning suddenly, leaping out at me from the filthy morass of strangers, I catch sight of a brow, the corner of a lip, a cheek-bone, the back of a neck, hook of nose, that matches his, almost. I see it, realise my mistake, thinking *Almost*. It's this *almost* that maddens me and soon I start grimacing to myself, then roaring out loud, laughing and laughing. *What am I thinking?* It's preposterous that he *shouldn't* be here. Even if it's only his nose or his collar-bone that's here, it's still him. But the lie soon makes my heart ache.

I feel eyes upon me so I run off down the street, cutting crossways to hide for a moment, hating the thought of their fangs on my bruised neck, wanting to keep his imprint there just a little while longer, not much longer, just for a little while. Thinking *How long will the echo of him and me crashing against one another last? How soon will it be gone? And then what? What will I do then?* I realise that I have to find a way, there has to be a way to sustain the sound of him and me together. I can't just be left with my own over-hot mind clattering against itself, wearing itself out until the echo of him gets lost altogether beneath the grim clang of this crowded, buzzing isolation.

Out of breath and panting like a sick cat, I lean against a filthy doorway for a moment until I'm sure there's no one around. But when I look up, I see someone watching me from across the street. It's an old woman, about seventy-five, delirious on crap booze, listing like an Atlantic liner, almost sinking beneath the troughs of effort as she struggles to make sense of the child-jumble of dusky shapes in the street around her. I know the woman is me, fifty years from now, but instead of neatly remembering, I shut my eyes to this certain future and lie down in a comfortable spot on the sidewalk and breathe deeply the scent of shit and wet stone. Nauseous with chance, I suspect my fear, wondering which way it will push me, at this moment knowing only the fear, not what it will make me do. For a second, I use my eyes and nothing else. I spy great things overhead: clouds staggering across the tiny gap between building tops, vapour trails funnelling through the remaining blue, the sickly glow of an invented dusk as the neon billboards, gangrenous street lights and anaemic office strips pop on all over the city, blinding out the stars with one heavenwards stab of incredible light.

~

So we're standing on the threshold of her room and the Swissman is hesitating in the darkness behind me, his gangly figure becoming gradually indiscernible as he begins to fumble away along the corridor towards the far part of the house where he'll be sleeping, and I'm wishing he'd just keep on walking all the way back to New York, all that way and beyond, just leave me alone with this lovely little creature, but he's hesitating like the idiot mosquitoes outside the windows at dusk, just waiting for the right moment to interrupt my sleep.

Time suddenly compresses and it's as though the air gets tight around us. I'd swear she felt it too. Beyond the window, the pool is lit up, beaming out an unnatural turquoise, a rectangle of fluid luminescence. I can't bear to look at her. I know the light breeze from off the sea which is making the pool shiver will mean that her face is shining like an angel in the trembling light, so I don't look at her, it'll be too much.

This maybe all happens in a few seconds, no more than that, perhaps it's even less. We're standing there in the doorway and suddenly I see everything for the first time, the house I've lived in for the last forty-five years, the broad cedars and Scots pines, the whole look of the place new-seeming to me as I stand there with her. We've not said anything yet. Then I think she says something like 'Thank you for making my bed' but all I hear is 'bed' and I'm thinking about what she'd do if I came back here just as soon as that skinny Swissman has got lost, if I came back here and just slipped into bed beside her. I can't get beyond that moment of just getting into bed beside her long, cool limbs beneath the sheets, just getting next to her is all, because I'm made suddenly nauseous like I'm actually going to vomit at the thought of being away from her now she's here, so I don't dare let myself get beyond just slipping into bed beside her, just taking it slow, one thing at a time, nice and easy, so's not to frighten her. But of course it's me I'm frightened of. Getting all shaken up about some girl, just having dirty thoughts about her, I tell myself, that's all it is, just me getting dirty on her and where's the surprise in that? After all, she's a beautiful girl and I'm still a man, however decrepit I might be.

So we're standing there in the doorway. She says, 'Bed,' I say, 'Sleep well,' something like that, then, my mind going suddenly BAM, like sucked-silent air after a thunderclap, I kiss her real polite, just once, on her cheek, my right hand touching her briefly at the base of her spine, feeling the heat of her skin through that thin white dress she's wearing. Stepping away from her I'm convinced she'll notice me reeling like a drunk, but she turns, murmuring, 'Good-night,' I think, before going back into her room while I walk off, following the Swissman (who is still only a few yards away, in fact, it all happened so quick he hadn't got far), and all I can think is *fuck fuck fuck* over and over like a baby's howling, the whole thing going fast and hot inside my head.

That was the first time I touched her. I'd been meticulous about not letting myself touch her before, even when I handed her her drink. I'd wanted to wait and see. So now I knew – like I didn't before – that she was the one and everything else had been something different entirely, absolutely unimportant by comparison, shabbily lustful and little more than clumsy when set against this sensation, of what? I didn't dare aim at it with a name just yet but how I hated her at that moment. How could she do this to me? What gave her the right to ruin me like that?

It would be night now, only there is no night in the city with its whorish glare prodding the eyes and the arses of the people who scatter beneath its gaudy sky, looking for trade, some myth of human contact, a fuck, a look, an avoidance, whatever they can lay their bony fingers on, eerily rapacious in the soup of neon and implausible gloom, all of them strangers, just like me. I hate everyone I set eyes on, straightforwardly, for not being him. I curse all of them, myself included. When the sun has gone down, the shadows stay put, closed down over the cityscape like an awning: clack, thud, a meaningless rotation of the world.

I lean for a cool moment against the wall of a building, heaving the aroma of piss into my lungs as I watch the people rush about from one street to the next, without purpose but filled with intent to cross the next minute, hour, day, year, just to get to it and beyond it, never thinking whether they want it or not, just to get there and beyond is all, some dementia whirring through their muscles like a tic they need no excuse for. So they hurry by, shutting their hungry mouths like traps, wanting only to avoid discovering what the flesh of the world tastes like, terrified to risk an end to boredom, the neat crack of clear-sightedness at the back of the neck.

I take one look at all of this and head off to a bar I know where the girls put their scarred tits in your face for five dollars and Leroy, the barman, recognises me from when I was here last week with the Swissman. He looks surprised, then disgusted when he sees that I'm here by myself, but cheers up when I slip him ten for a double, drink it standing up and leave before he's had chance to decide whether he should pick out a girl for me. 'You got a licence for those legs yet?' he manages to croak as I slam the glass back down on the bar and head out the door, feeling better already, giving him a cheery wave goodbye, on top of the world.

I'd only been in there a few minutes, or perhaps hours, I forget, but when I get back out in the street things have changed already. Ruffled like black crows, sexless figures dissolve into dimly lit bars. They spit at one another, laughing their heads off, the stones in their eyes tumbling about, clicking wildly from one scene to the next, looking for nothing in particular.

I loiter and try not to stare. Soon enough I feel eyes at my back, quickly followed by fingers and a tongue on my neck. 'You dance with me?' seems appropriate enough, so I go with the man, avoiding looking at him even when he slams me back against the dripping brickwork, oozing saliva on to his shirt, stiff with dry-cleaning. I look at his face, noticing the similarities, thinking perhaps this is the way to keep the echo of him upon me, or, failing that, to destroy it utterly, recreate it in some stranger's image, really not much different from his, how could it be? How could it? Wondering keeps me here, watching his face for signs, thinking *Perhaps this is the way?* The hungry acquisition of each bright moment significant merely as fuel for some kind of motion, change of whatever kind, a means of escape from who I was before, that vision now fast-fading in the gleam of night. This is, at least, the way *he* lived, pulling around himself the various sounds and sights of the world like a cloak of legitimacy, calling it invention because of its ostensible, word-infested strangeness to himself, so why shouldn't I? Imitation is one sure way of staying pressed up close to him. And might it not in fact be the right way to live after all, the fascination of the myth which can be made to fit. *Isn't that what I'm doing right now?* I ask myself, looking attentively into the man's eyes, already beginning to suspect my mistake, which of course is hardly surprising, only I didn't realise quite how soon I would see it. But there's something triumphant in the wild disparity between who I am and who this sorry man is seeing. It could even be hilarious, the lunatic mismatch of body to person, were it not so unshakeably true. He gets put off by my laughter and jams a fist delicately into my mouth for me to suck, so I can't help but inhale the obsessive soap from his fingers as he mutters sweet things against my ear and then tries to buy me dinner saying, 'You were really wild back then,' looking confused, as well he might, when I kick him in the shins because I'm disappointed to tears by the simple fact that it's not *him*, though it could almost be him, the way he crumples to the floor being not dissimilar to the way *he* had fallen to the wide bed as I clung around his neck like a ruby choker, raw with lust.

But it's not him, of course it's not him, so I stroll off through the unsteady night, aiming listlessly for the next bar, disparaged by the inevitability of the hollow roaring still drowning out the light in my heart, bullied to bruising-point by my violent mind. Just before I go inside, I stare up through the cracks between the buildings at the sky, beautiful with sallow reflections of the city, and wonder how long it will be before I can forget him. Feeling the weight of possibility lifting off my heart, releasing it as though from the tolerable certainty of a velvet vice, leaving me with one impossible longing, a raw yearning which empties me of all other sensation. So I stare and stare until rivers flood out of my eyes, drowning the people who jostle around me in the street, as urgent as I am to get the alkali inside their stinking guts so they can cower, unseen, in the dark room of oblivion, if just for a while.

~

But you can't turn over almost seventy-five years of hard living and unhopefulness with just one touch, that's the way I saw it as I walked back to my room that night. I remember, I went outside to stand for a moment by the pool, watching the glassy surface wrinkle and shift in the slight breeze which carried the scent of pine trees, warmed by the hot day still in the earth's thoughts, not yet ready to be forgotten. Summer is like that here. Smells linger. Even the days become unnaturally protracted, the diminishing light, hesitant at the edges of your vision, making you feel like you're on an island, not part of the massive bulk of America at all.

As I stand, barefoot, on the edge of the pool, her light goes out. I stare at the now dark rectangle of the window and have the strong sensation of her eyes burning out from the black room, watching me hanging around outside, so I pick up the long-armed pool cleaner and scoop some imaginary bit of muck off the clean surface of the water, feeling like an idiot. But hell, I live here, not her, I tell myself, I can do what I like.

It seems as though everyone around abouts must have gone to sleep. It's always quiet, but not usually this quiet. Then my ears get sensitive to the other sounds of the night. Not the people, the cars, the blundering animals thrashing around for food through the undergrowth, dense and protective around this place, no, not those sounds. It's like I can hear the sounds of the earth itself, like the soil is settling after the day's heat, the tree roots curling more tightly beneath the imbalance of their overhead burdens to keep them from falling. I'm wondering why I've never stood out here at night like this before, it's so pleasurable. Then I begin to wonder what I'm doing out here by myself, with half a mind to go wake her up and tell her about the trees and the soil sinking into sleep, but realising that she'll think I'm a crazy lunatic if I do that. Then, swaying slightly, I remember how much we just drank and how fast. *So I must be drunk*, I tell myself. What am I thinking of, imagining she'd want to be woken up and invited outside to stand like this in the dark with me on an ordinary night in summer. Not even like it's the fourth of July with fireworks or anything, just an ordinary night like any other. So I go back inside, trying to walk noisily, slam a few doors, give the house some of its familiar sounds back, get rid of the sound of the soil and the groaning trees which is becoming oppressive like heat around my head. Last time I drink that much, that's what it is, the alcohol, and I'm not getting any younger.

I can't delay going back to England for much longer, so I tell myself: just one more night alone in the city and I'll be ready to go back, just one more night before my other life resumes. Today is too soon, that's all it is. I need more time. I have to put some space between then and now so that I can mark out the place where I will keep him inside me, safe from the harm of time and change, because soon, many years too soon, I will be somewhere else entirely, a different country even, and all of this will cut deep like madness, swamping me with disbelief. So when it's night, I head downtown to a place I know where the barman, an ex-boxer, tells anyone who cares to hear about his passion for Baudelaire. What he doesn't mention is that he spits into the beer if he doesn't like you. He tells great stories, though, and it's nice to listen to him drawling on, his eyes gleaming like ripe flints underwater.

But this time he avoids me, looking suspiciously at my crazy eyes, which I can't stop from sliding across towards the bottles lined up like tarts at a bus-stop, indolent beneath the ugly hot lights. He keeps the whiskys coming, though, for which I'm grateful, slipping glasses up and down the bar towards people as though it were a factory, and you've got to be quick to catch your drink before the next person on the conveyor belt gets it and guzzles it down.

Tonight there's rain outside beyond the greenish neon sign and inside there's the cloying stink of steaming clothes and damp flesh. To pass the time before tomorrow I play a game, pretending I'm *him*, just to see what happens, thinking *Maybe this is the way to keep him close beside me*, close enough for me to smell the hot skin damp against me, taste the tongue-roughened hairs across his body and feel the emphatic earthwards falling weight of him as he dives into me, looking for the dark places along the bottom of the filthy pit which somehow, against the odds, we both looked at in grim unison, though briefly and now so long ago, since grounded in a time already past. But I have to keep shutting my eyes because whenever I look up beyond the rim of my glass, which I try to keep at eye level, my chin propped against the bar, I catch sight of myself in the mirror behind the bottles and it's patently me, not him at all, despite the drink, despite my endlessly rerunning in my mind's eye his smile, his lips, his broad chest, his wild-man's soft shock of white hair, his hard cock

45

pressed proudly against my belly as if it were my own.

Then just as I slip towards the cusp of forgetting that I'm playing a game I feel surreptitious fingers against my back, a tentative, searching pressure. I do not stir and even quit swaying, steadying myself against the bar, eyes wide open now, wondering. And there are definitely fingers, softly nudging in between my shoulder-blades, and I look up, bringing the woman behind me into focus in the mirror's reflection. She's beautiful and tragic-looking, with pale skin that is luminous against the spider-crawlings of her black hair swooshing over her face through the darkness as she leans towards me, her inquisitive fingers finding a way inside the back of my dress to print little patterns up and down my spine with her long nails, scratching me gently as though I were a cat and my back were a velvety ear, malleable and nice to touch. She's talking to a man as she touches me and I notice her other hand put down her drink on the bar, then get lost in the muss of gloom which swallows up his cock below waist height so no one notices his quick satisfaction. He grins broadly, as well he might, but doesn't seem to notice her other hand slipping down between my thighs to catch my pleasure unawares, facing me now, but sideways on and not looking down so she doesn't see my look of sudden recognition as I realise that she is just the kind of girl *he* would've liked, as though playing at being him I've become him in some brief, parallel universe. She's licking her other hand now before she reaches round to pick up her drink again, making that man she's with drool with renewed interest and rub himself up against her like a filthy dog, trying to drag her away and out into the street so he can get inside her again. And it's as though this lovely little couple are acting like a tableau vivant arranged just for my pleasure, so perfectly timed and placed that I know I'm going to have to restrain myself from clapping when she's done, if he doesn't drag her away by the squealing roots of her hair first.

She can read my mind, because before she slaps down her glass on the bar, scudding it off along the polished ice-track surface towards the Baudelaire-loving barman, and even before she's jauntily picked off her leopard-spotted coat from the rack beside the door, and many delightful minutes before she's swept out of here to the sound of my stamping and sobbing *Enough! For the love of Christ!* without even one backward glance to see the destruction she's left in her shuddering wake as she sails off through the night to whichever harbour she chooses, before all of this, many minutes before all of this, with her scarlet fingertips bared like fangs, she brings me to the last trembling point of pleasure, and it's all I can do to stop myself from wailing wetly like a crazy maenad at the sweet symmetry of my present situation.

~

I'm inside the house now. All the lights are on on this side of the building. See, I have a central lighting system alongside all the regular switches for each individual light, because being so remote I figured it'd be a good way to scare off burglars or anyone else who decided to creep around the place at night, give 'em a shock with 500 watts of electric light. So I walk around the place, neatening it up before I turn in for the night. I clear away the glasses and bottles, and take them over to the sink. Then I notice one of them has the faintest trace of pale-coloured lipstick, so I know it's hers. I don't know why I do this, but I can't resist putting the glass to my lips and licking along the now-cold rim, cleaning off the colour like a busy cat, smiling at my foolishness like a kid caught with his hand in the cookie jar. It tastes faintly of vanilla, powdery and unfamiliar, and I wonder whether she likes this taste, what thought goes through her mind when she licks her lips, tasting it like I'm tasting it now. Knowing there's no one to catch me, I'm able to smile at myself, thinking what a crazy thing to do, not questioning why I did it, washing the glass up along with the rest, feeling almost like my usual self again as I establish order in the house. Before I go upstairs, I check that all the windows and doors are tight against the mosquitoes, then, when I'm satisfied that everything's in order, I go upstairs.

The house is built in the shape of a straight-edged, open 'C' and, apart from the roof, is made entirely of white-painted timber, with a veranda running right around it a few feet above ground level, which is where I like to sit and read in summertime, following the sunlight as it travels across the building. The corridor along the top floor has two large windows in it. They look out over the pool towards the other side of the house. I pretend I'm not doing this, but I can't help myself taking a quick squint over to the window of the room where she's sleeping. The light is off and the room could almost be empty, it looks just the same as it always does but I stare at it a little while, imagining her tan skin against the smooth cotton sheets and her red hair licking over the pillow like flames. I wonder how she looks when she sleeps, what position she lies in, whether she likes to sleep alone, or if it makes her nervous. I realise that I don't know whether she has a boyfriend or even if she's married. The Swissman didn't say either

50

way, but she must have someone, I reason, girls like that always do.

Stop this, you old fool, I'm thinking to myself. Not that thought exactly, more like a rumbling non-thought pushing me in the direction of forgetfulness, blank nullity. I take deep breaths, trying to imagine with each in-breath that I'm re-inhaling the old familiar air of my life up until this point, at least, before I met her, when I knew what was going on with the world. Even if I did despise what I knew and found it disappointing beyond words and all grim expectation, at least then I had expectations, even if they were bitter ones, not like this hideous quaking hopefulness without reason or cause. So now I think of my emptying-filling lungs as my vile salvation through habit, the stale air become a stubbornly taken placebo. *Don't even think about it*, I say to myself, trying not to give up thinking about it absolutely, at least not just yet, because what else can I do, with someone so lovely to think about and her only yards away, God help me.

In the bathroom things are a little better because in there I can't help but see the wrinkles, sagging skin, wild white hair and all the other signs of implausibility. Not that I'm in bad shape for a man of my age, coming up to seventy-six next spring if I make it that far, but I'm old, there's no getting away from it, I'm just old and that's the honest truth. *Think about something else*, I tell myself, *how hard can that be? Just take a look.* So I decide to have a shave: my last resort at times like this. *Not that there ever has been a time like this*, my mind replies before I can stop it.

So I get busy with all my shaving paraphernalia, and pretty soon I start to feel the soft swell of nervous excitement. *A woman is waiting* is what shaving just before bed can mean, someone dewy-limbed from bathing, fragile-skinned and wary of abrasions. Coupled with visions of an immaculate slumberous death, unexpected midnight disturbances, cleaning up after a long day's work, a test of dwindling aptitude for delicate tasks, forcing my mind to switch from thoughts uninvited, like now, like thoughts of *her* – all this plays a part. At the very least, shaving before sleep creates in me an overwhelming feeling of readiness. Even if all I'm ready for is sleep, at least that's something that isn't going to catch me absolutely unawares, I say to myself, grimacing at my reflection in the mirror.

Now the water is just right, nice and hot, almost scalding. I wet the naked cut-throat blade so it slips across my limp skin, held tight to make the bristles stand up straight. I don't want to slash my face to ribbons, like it's so easy to do with these blades which will peel your face off like a tangerine if you're not careful. But you get the best shave from razors like this and the risk makes me concentrate, maybe the only moments some days that I do concentrate this hard on anything, so it's no bad thing. I use The King of Oils, my preferred brand, I get closer that way and it leaves my skin feeling easy, not like some soaps and foams which sting and make it feel taut and fragile. There are many advantages to using oil to shave with. It smells good, too, not a strong perfume, but nice.

All my wives, without exception, tried to get me to use some other method of shaving. I'd have to lock them out of the bathroom just in order to perform this simple task. Otherwise, given half a chance and an unlocked door, they'd prance around behind me, squinting and chastising. 'You only use that fancy oil to make me mad,' Joany would say. 'You think it's so brave, wielding a deadly blade at your face like that,' was Lucille's line, her snarl an accusation of crimes graver than merely shaving. Jackie, on the other hand, with her eye-rolling antics, cared the least of all. She just wanted to meddle. Respectful to the point of servitude about my work, she imagined that anything else I did was to be regarded with suspicion, never believing I might have preferences of any kind, even about something as simple as a shave. But it was Sabrina's anger that cut the deepest: it felt like a premonition edging towards desire. 'If you want to kill yourself, go right ahead, just not in front of the child.' And I knew that she hated me, merely tolerated the boy. Unsurprising, then, that now, wifeless, I should enjoy shaving so much.

I fold up the razor and stand for a moment, inspecting my face in the mirror. Behind me the room is in darkness, making my head appear almost luminous in the glow of the strip light above the sink. I take in the lines and shadows of age scrawled all over my face, overwhelmed for a moment of what could almost be curiosity verging on shock. It is as though the last few minutes of frantic reappraisal of wives and lives now past was merely my mind's efficient and spontaneous way of clearing the path for thoughts of *her*, leaving space for nothing else whatsoever but these now clear visions which float sweetly through my mind. I watch my face take on an aspect weirdly serene, is how it seems, calmly certain almost, though my guts are still twisted up with defiance, reluctant through what is doubtless no more than habit to jettison everything that has gone before her. Because that's what this means, I tell myself, that's what it means to let her in at this eleventh hour and probably mistakenly too, without any sign from her at all, just this animal-simple combination of my own fear and regret for all the idiot mistakes I've made.

So I move backwards suddenly, away from the light, hidden once again in the evasive gloom, plodding the corridor unseen, not yet wanting to own the expression of feverish surprise which I just saw dancing all over my face for the first time in God knows how long, and which now still trips along insistent behind me as I shuffle off to bed alone, making like it is just any old night of the year and I have the house to myself as before.

Things will look better at forty thousand feet I tell myself as I swill my guts out with booze in the airport bar. But of course things don't look any better, only darker, more confined, less plausible, and I start to click my tongue against my brain in irritation as this great hunk of metal I'm in hurtles through the sky. Soon enough I drift in and out of a despairing whisky sleep, wondering when someone will come to arrest me or throw me off the plane to the wolves which gnaw the sky and wag their tails at the sea beneath, chasing stars as jackdaws do when they mess around with the dragonflies at dusk. But no one comes. I look like anyone else. It's only my secret insides which are heaving with newness. Inside my skull a razor-blade has been busy with a precise intention of eye peeling: see everything, but from now on be able to do nothing whatsoever *but* see, disengaged sight something horrific when the world is so full of other happy chances which now, by meeting him, I cannot take. Of course, the mystery of broken isolation is more apalling than it has any right to be. It cuts to the heart and the wound suppurates and yawns ever wider, festering.

There are no clouds outside the tiny windows, only the endless, fading blue, occasional vapour trails and, soon enough, a sky the colour of freshly spilled Quink as the lights in the plane snap off all at once and we are supposed to sleep. But the sudden darkness makes me wide awake and I listen to the sighs and grunts of the packed-in people, muttering beneath the profound roar of the engines.

I get up and lurch to the loo at the back of the plane to squeeze some piss out of myself, dangling my head in my hands, before standing up and looking at my face in the leprous mirror. I might as well be wearing a Hallowe'en mask, because I can't make myself recognise the freakish stranger in the glass, even though I try, squinting and screwing up my eyes to catch my face off guard, seize it unawares and shake some of my old life back into it. I am merely someone else now, although the face itself still fits to the exact same pattern as before. But there's nothing I can do about it, however much I might gag at the helplessness of the transformation. I have killer's eyes. And although it's only a crime against myself, I'm blatantly guilty of it, like a dog caught snacking on a butcher's foot, bitten off with a neat snap! of its jaws, precisely, at

57

the ankle bone just above the Achilles heel. Perhaps it's the night that has concealed me, or the strange city where one madman is as bad as the next. But this can't last, all this unfamiliarity. Soon enough someone will notice and I'll be put somewhere out of sight so I can scratch myself in solitude and remember him for ever in peace amen.

I get back to my seat just as we start the slow float back to earth, in my nostrils the reek of booze and damp disappointment. Voices behind me say: 'I should think Bournemouth would be nice in June. You can swim there.' 'I need to have words with my son.' 'Well, *have* them!' And as I look out at the edge of dawn slicing its way towards the diminished land, I imagine a sky-borne mouth gaping hilariously as I scatter empty whisky bottles, hurling them overboard like a banshee at Whitsuntide.

So I shut my eyes to the sight, far beneath us, of London, gleaming despite itself in the early morning light which creeps feverishly across the fields, hedgerows, gasworks, factories, mysterious offices with dumb-struck windows and hideous rivers nudging their way through the changing land, sustained on some depthless dream of the sea.

~

Thud thud thud, it's becoming worse, not better, beating against the inside of my head so I can't sleep and I'm thinking how I don't remember anything this bad, not since the war, can you believe? It's not a pain exactly, just a sense of vague foreboding like before a rain of shells, and the only image in my head is of her face, smiling and laughing, looking at me and laughing in a way that makes me suspect she must find me pitiful.

I turn over and over in bed like a pancake getting overcooked, not able to sleep even for a minute. It's like my body is fighting the magnetic pull of the idea I had earlier, my brief thought that I'd just go over there to where she is and slip into bed beside her, not try anything on, just slip into bed beside her, saying hush hush hush hush hush like you do to a frightened animal or a squalling baby to get it quiet. My limbs feel like they've just taken me on a twenty-mile run, they're aching so bad with the effort of not getting up and going over to her. What a mess, I'm thinking, I've got to turn this one around, she's just a stupid girl after all, why the fuss? And my thoughts are racing about like dizzy bees smashing themselves against a bare light bulb, always whacking back to the same point which is her, the one heat-filled point of concentrated imagining filling up my mind with light. But light which burns, pressing up against the pumping veins in my brain, forcing the pressure, so now my mind feels fit to burst, like a water hydrant in the tight heat of midsummer.

I see her suddenly in a flash like wildfire, her red hair blazing, her rosy lips smiling, laughing at me, as the intense heat she gives off, in one casual, deliberate flourish of violent certainty, razes to the ground the entire edifice of my life up until this moment. She lifts her young smiling face up to mine, giving me a look of simple admission, as much as to say *It's obvious this would happen, don't you think*? As though the blame for laying bare my entire life rests with me, not her. But it *is* her, I tell myself, gritting my ant-cracking teeth like a blackened forest animal might, one that has become so used to the musky darkness and damp, slow solitude of its forage for food, the easy hunt along familiar tracks, that any disruption merely stuns, bewildering it, so that it stands in the bright clearing, alone, pathetically snarling at the vacant daylight.

It's only natural that soon I begin to hate her. But I didn't know just how quickly nor how much I'd start to be angry with her for putting this hex on me, making me sleepless and dissatisfied. Suddenly it comes upon me, a dark smog of hate for the way she's almost fooled me into feeling soft about her. What the fuck! So now in my mind I'm going through to her room, shouldering open the door. She'll have left it open for sure, the whore, she'll have been waiting for me. Women always wait like that, passive, bovine, quick to startle, slow to react. I'll crash the door open, rush into the bedroom where she's lying, probably asleep by now. I'll be quick before she realises what's happening and before she can stop me I'll be on her, entering her sleep like a sudden nightmare that leaves her wet and wanting it harder than she's ever had it, right inside her so she's not sure whether she's crying for more or crying for me to stop, she won't even know herself it'll be so sudden, so unexpected, but still what she really wanted, just like all women. And she won't cry out, won't be able to, because I'll have one hand over her mouth, the other holding her wrists tight and easily above her head, she's so weak. It'll be quick and hard, and no one will come to stop it, no one will even hear. When I'm done I will laugh at her like she laughed at me. What else does she expect?

I sneak into the empty house feeling thievish and sly. I stand in the hallway for a moment, breathing in the remembered air, sweet with dust and sudden familiarity. I think *Now my life will resume. Look, all the pieces fit, so why shouldn't it?* He is not here with me and nor will he ever be. He exists in another life altogether, a life which is branded inside the deepest part of me whether I want it there or not. And I know I want it there, a talisman for the restless violence of my jumping mind, aflame with visions which until meeting him I suspected were no more than glimpses of ludicrous isolation. I tell myself I feel nothing but gratitude, intense gratitude, that he has shown me the perfect way to protect myself from the numb threat of happiness, the state that stultifies and breeds contentment. Happiness, I remind myself, is something which I can sweep across my skin like magic embrocation, warming me with child promises of forgetfulness. But I will not forget, of course.

There is a note propped up against a flower-filled vase on the hall table which reads: 'Welcome home, darling!' and I stare at the piece of paper, fighting off the urge to smash my head against the wall like a confused moth. *But I'm not confused! Never been clearer,* I reason to myself, starting to feel almost jaunty like a captive bird suddenly caught in a slipstream of wind might feel, never realising that it could go so fast, for a moment not even caring where it goes to, just going, even if this means the final obliterating slam into a wall, that doesn't matter because the speed itself, for those moments of intense motion, is more than enough to make its tiny trembling soul see the flash of possibility, setting fire to its entire life, showing it that things can be absolutely different from the way it imagined.

So I take my bags upstairs and put things away where they belong, hanging my clothes up in the cupboard like sloughed skins. And as the day fades into afternoon, I don't exactly start to skip as I go about the house *where I live with my husband* but I feel a sense of acute detachment which has the appearance perhaps of serenity as I stroll around the familiar rooms naming things as I pass them, gathering up all the lovely facts to take a good look at this life I have which still exists. Just take a look! I even have letters waiting for me in a neat stack on the kitchen table, and there are green trees and a bluish sky outside the window and the ticking clock and the chiming church bells *clang* on the quarter-hour, and everything's just fine and almost precisely how it was before.

Soon enough it is dark outside and I take a bath, do my hair, put on lipstick and a dress, and when my husband comes home there are cooking smells from the kitchen, bottles of wine chilling in the fridge, and I am happy to see him and he is happy to see me.

A domestic scene:

HUSBAND (*embracing wife*) Darling! Oh it's so good to see you. I've missed you, you know.
WIFE (*lifting her lips to his*) Have you really? Oh and I've missed you too. Look, special dinner. You hungry?
HUSBAND (*steering her towards the door*) Never mind about that. It's been two weeks. The food can wait.

So I watch all this going on alongside me in close-up, as though from behind the watery glass of a telescope, focused into immaculate but absolutely unaffecting clarity, and really it's all very charming. I look at it with an overwhelming sense of nostalgia like an ancient dog remembering great bones of its youth in a dream where it twitches on a rug beside the fire, its legs running madly after the fading visions of marrow and flesh.

The lights are dimmed in the bedroom as we tumble upstairs and there are newly laundered sheets on the bed. Entering the room is like watching a replay of something easy and familiar, and his hands upon my body have no effect whatsoever. He removes my clothes and presses himself keenly against me. I watch myself, faintly surprised that I feel so little, neither repulsion nor desire, comfort or pity, hot or cold. Everything is merely straightforward and unengaging. There is a clock beside the bed which ticks and whirs as the minutes click by and he tells me how happy he is that I seem to be so glad to see him and I say, truthfully, 'Yes, but I am glad to see you!' This seems to please him, though not as much as my wet mouth around his cock, sucking him like a salty lollipop until his voice, become guttural, urges on his big hands across my body, exciting himself with the sound of his thickly croaked-out desires, his eyes roving in the half-light across my skin, seeing beneath him the same body as before. I'm curious to see if he can tell the difference. He can't. There is no difference! I conclude, triumphant in this shoddy deceit. Nothing happened after all and now I can resume. At least, my body can resume its familiar trudge through the days, just carry on as before, enduring fiercely the unruptured flow from then to now.

But I am worlds apart from myself and when he plunges into me again and again as though he's seen the gold glinting at the bottom of the pool and has to have it, I suspect he imagines that in fucking me he erases everything within me that is not him, and deep inside I am laughing and laughing as the tears stream through my guts like fire, burning through me until my whole body is ablaze with memory and the impossibility of this dear deceived man's ever having reached me, crash as he might through the barricades of my fathomless desire, now no more than an impenetrable longing, impossible to satisfy.

As though from a great height, I watch him crawling around inside me, oblivious, and I am almost jealous. When he is done, I understand things with such indelible clarity I want to cheer, and tear off through the streets brandishing my little discovery like a gleaming knife, waving it in the faces of strangers who stare, unmoved.

The discovery is merely what I already knew to be true: that, like *him*, I have two lives, not one. And as he slips out of me I barely feel the nauseating pull of despair, dragging me back to the wretched pit in my mind where my imagination rips through time and impossibility to live, really to live. Because for a brief moment, but still it's enough of a moment, these two lives hang in delicate equilibrium, perfectly balanced, giving me just enough time to see how things will be as I survey the long stretch of years before me with calm wonder and a burgeoning quake of noiseless, bright-eyed excitement as the void casually opens up beside me.

~

Around four-thirty in the morning I wake up suddenly. I stare up at the ceiling. Now this is the same ceiling I've woken up underneath for over thirty years but this morning it's different. I stare at it to try to see why, to see what's changed. Perhaps some more paint has started to crumble, it might need fixing, but the same cracks are there in the same familiar formation. There's not much light at this time in the morning, but what light there is I like to have coming into my bedroom as soon as it's ready. You could call it a pathological fear of endless night – I could never live wherever it is that they get entire weeks of night. Forget it. All my wives had a problem with my need for light as soon as possible in the mornings. 'Sleep under the covers,' I'd say.

This morning, I don't know why, but things seem different. The light looks different. I think perhaps it has something to do with it coming up to a full moon tomorrow.

So I'm lying there, staring up at the ceiling, fully awake now, but my body restful, not yet ready to lift itself up and get out of bed. The light strengthens its pattern on my ceiling each second as I look at it, almost unblinking, not taking my eyes off it. It seems quiet outside but then I start to hear certain noises. First it's just a creak of wood against wood, like the house is resettling itself against the foundations. This lasts for maybe thirty seconds, then there's around a full minute of the usual sounds of silence which isn't silence at all, obviously, but wind and air and mechanical tickings from inside the house, electrical things with their own rhythms, nothing to do with me. Then there's a whooshing noise, unmistakably something diving into the pool, and I'm up in a flash, running out into the corridor to look out of the window to see what's going on.

It looks like a gold dagger, her naked body cutting through the deep part of the pool, right along the bottom, like a natural fish is how she looks. She swims the whole length of the pool and when she comes to the surface at the far end I realise I've held my breath for the same length of time, as though I've been underwater like she has. So I come up, gasping almost, sucking the air back into my hungry lungs, just like she does while she clings on to the edge, her thin shoulders heaving with the strain of being that long underwater at this time in the morning, like she's not used to doing it at all, which she probably isn't, of course.

It is unexpected, seeing her in the water like that. Without actually thinking about it, I'd imagined she was the sort of person to wake around noon, soft-limbed and vague until she's washed, done her hair, put on a nice dress, that kind of thing. But there she is, swimming at four-thirty in the morning, full of surprises. When I see her looking like a little fish I feel bad about hating her, but it's the only way, so I don't change my mind about that.

She swims out into the pool, dog-paddling backwards, treading water. Then she turns round and looks up at the house, straight up at the window where I am. I duck down but I'm convinced she must've seen me looking out at her. And the expression on her face! She's smiling this smile like an angel, not a grin exactly, but a smile containing all the joy and intense happiness that a grin might have, even though it's actually just a turned-up-at-the-edges kind of smile and quick as well, before she raises her arms above her head and goes straight down to the bottom of the pool like a firework, dead straight, vertically downwards, her flaming red hair streaming out behind her.

By now I've got out the way of the window so she can't see me. I'm behind the edge of the curtain, just looking at her with my right eye so I'm invisible. She gets to the bottom and twirls around a bit under the water, doing somersaults by the look of it, then she comes out, lifting a few feet clean out of the water with another big whooooosh like a mermaid, her red hair clinging to her head, most of it over her face now and almost covering her breasts which I catch a naked glimpse of as she comes above the surface. She has girl's breasts. Buoyant and rosy-nippled. Then she flips over on to her back and gets into a steady rhythm of swimming, paddling around slowly, methodically, from one end of the pool to the other, her breasts sticking right up, clean out of the water at every stroke. I can't see the expression on her face but she's sending out waves of happiness like a radiator sends out heat. I want to go and get next to her, get warm, pressed up against her. She's taking her time, swimming up and down, but I could watch her for ever. Then, suddenly, she flips over on to her stomach and does a few strokes of crawl to the edge and climbs out, her slender body turning silver in the grey light of dawn.

She's left a towel by the edge but she doesn't wrap herself up in it completely, just twists it around her waist like a man might, leaving those breasts exposed to the air like an Amazon setting out for a day's hunting. She tips her head upside down, then flings it upwards, sending the water flying off behind her. Up in the trees, even I can hear it from behind the closed window, the rooks screech all of a sudden, a sound mournful and petulant like they've been disturbed from sleep, and she turns to look up at the tree-tops where the sound came from. I look where she looks and, sure enough, the sky is suddenly filled with rooks put to flight but not going anywhere, settling back down after a minute, just showing they've been disturbed, and she's smiling again, even at this.

At breakfast, exactly two months after the weekend, my husband, engrossed as always in the morning papers, casually remarks: 'Look at this, oh, I am sorry, that writer chap you met in the summer has just popped his clogs. Have you seen the obits yet, darling?' He looks up briefly when he speaks *that writer chap has popped his clogs*, shaming me with the worn-out fear in his eyes, unmistakably becoming relief as I feign disinterest. 'What a pity, that is sad,' blindly leaving the room, locking myself in the bathroom upstairs until I hear, 'See you later, then, darling,' and the muted click of the front door. From behind the curtains I see him saunter away down the street. When he is out of sight I turn back into the room to watch it change as the morning staggers into afternoon, the persistent light like a reproach against unnoticed time. My hand reaching for the bottle marks the minutes until the brownish sliver the colour of decay, swilling seasickishly against the bottom of the glass, is almost gone and I go in search of more.

The locked cupboard beside the bookcase in

my study is also my secret store: a beautiful line-up of my favourite things, slurping brackishly like woozy back-lit oil fields. I haul out another bottle and watch the dusk creeping towards me across the building backs slewed squiffily at perplexing angles to the back of the house. I think about him. Of course I think about him. I imagine the final trip of haggard breath, hicking insubstantially in his gentle throat. I imagine that little gasp caught on the trip-wire of his last desire: to live. I think about all the grim faces at his funeral, none of them my own. I imagine relatives, friends, ex-wives and children, all unknown to me, yet violently diminished by his trembling, astonished declaration: *No one else but you has ever seen me.* I ask myself for the thousandth time: should I have stayed with him until the end? Was it wrong to leave as I did, wanting to show him that I was prepared to believe his fevered *It's all material*, even though I could tell that he had given up trusting in that ancient jailer's curse long ago. But I knew it was the most valuable thing I could give him: assurance that his life hadn't been lived as a mistake. So I left. I didn't look back. I didn't return to watch his horrified revelation, the moment when the full weight of his obdurate belief would surely collapse in on him, swamping him in doubt. There was a chance, by leaving when I did, that this moment would come so late as to be almost insignificant. And with his hands soft and admiring about my throat, his teeth bared against the words, *You must be my angel of death, coming here like this, with so little time*, I was able merely to join in his despair, knowing the entire, brief union to be too simple and sure to cling to like some rockish child, hungry for ignorance and illusion: there was nothing we could have held on to that wouldn't have dissolved to dust as we held it. So it was right that I left when I did. At least, this is what I tell myself, missing him as a stunned, stubborn beast might, still waiting for its legs to catch up with the shock of sudden speed, the race downhill.

Unlit, the house takes on a threatening aspect, so I pull on a coat and head out of the door, thumping off down the street into the welcoming night, the half-full bottle clanging heavily at my side. I walk. The road leans downwards, weaving continuously with no sense of getting to anywhere other than somewhere else exactly like itself. There is a huge moon tonight, vast above the rooftops. It gleams wetly into the private lives of strangers, reminding them of their undiscovered *doppelgängers* who lurk, similarly, inevitably, on the other side of town. With the night comes an insidious fog, creeping along beside me, tightening its fingers around the nape of my neck until my throat aches. I fall into step behind first one man and then another, trying out their footfalls for familiarity until I find one which matches my own and I pad along behind him until he turns round abruptly and, at precisely the same pace, walks towards me, his battleship eyes bearing me down like a maniac.

Later, arriving home around one, sneaking into the silent house, my husband's sleeping breaths booming unheard around my ears, I absolve myself beneath a steaming shower, thinking: *This is how he lived.* The night-time wanderings, the forgettable forging of flesh upon flesh, the endless search for minute avatars with unfamiliar people, the undead hope, each second obfuscated by disappointed desire and always against reason, but still, the hope! Always the hope and at all costs.

That night the howl of the feral dogs makes my flesh thicken and cringe. It disgusts me, turning me red-rotten inside my head as I long to squirm with them, fang-drip my way deep into the mud and shit where they shuffle together insensibly. Of course, he found this charming, seeing in me the twin to his own clever filth. But how lightly I anticipated his death.

~

The next thing she does surprises me even more. She rushes into the house and then emerges a minute later, now wearing a kind of slip, still barefoot, but with a towel wound turban-style around her wet hair and with one of the large stripy blankets from off the bed thrown across her shoulders. She's carrying a large leather-bound notebook, tucked under her arm, and she's looking wild-eyed, staring up at the trees as if she's seen a ghost. She hunkers down on the ground, cross-legged, grinning to herself like a madwoman. Then it's like a scene in church, where instead of communion someone receives a blessing from the priest, making them suddenly still like a bird calmed by its being trapped. She's just like that, not stopped, exactly, but suddenly at peace as she glances up for a moment at the broad, high trees where the rooks have now settled again.

It is then that she starts to write, on her face an expression of indescribable serenity and concentration. And it's as though the vision of her sitting there beneath the tree, confident as a child, precisely as she is right now, boyish and self-contained, somehow completes a picture I haven't for many years had the courage to imagine. And although my mind is still twisted up with its desperate *Not now, not yet*, I know that it's no use. I feel like someone has hit me between the eyes with a sledgehammer for the second time in only eleven hours, because I realise that she's just like me and for the first time in my life I've met my match. The only thing is, it's just about sixty years too late.

So I quit looking at her and go back to the bedroom to lie down, well aware that I'll not sleep but lying down all the same, knowing it doesn't matter anyway whether I look at her or not because she's burnt into my mind now, like a cattle brand stamped across my entire sorry life. However hard I try, I can't call up anything else to usurp her image. She's the only thing in my head. I lie there for about two hours, until seven-fifteen, which I figure is a perfectly normal time to get up at, so up I get, walking along the corridor close to the wall so I don't get tempted to look out of the window to see if she's still there, and get to the bathroom without seeing her. I stand under the shower, turning it hot and cold alternately, which is how I like it in the mornings. Evenings I prefer it just warm, I find it more soothing that way, but in the morning the alternation of temperatures is invigorating. I'm under the water, still thinking about her, but by this time I'm telling myself that I'll soon come to terms with it, so what the hell.

I catch sight of myself in the mirror. I look at my crazy white hair and at my old body, sagging more and more by the minute, loose bits of flesh turning yellow, almost gangrenous, putrid-seeming, and I'm glad to my heart that I'm an old man. I stand there under the cold water, watching my shrivelled old self, not too bad for my age, but there's no avoiding the fact that I'm shrivelled, and I reason like this: a girl like that couldn't possibly feel for an old man like me what I feel for her, with her so young and lovely. It's merely out of the question. Not something to feel blue about. Just a simple impossibility. Like a fact about the universe, something to do with the speed of light or whatever, and I find it oddly comforting that I've realised this now, so soon, rather than stewing about her, as though there were any chance of anything whatsoever happening, ever. I look at myself in the mirror and I even start to feel quite roguish, like I'm one of those undignified old men with a girl on either arm, too ridiculous to be even plausible, not me at all. That's what it would be like, I admonish myself, if I were to let it get out of hand, not that it would even get that far. Whichever way you look at it, it'd be an absurd future and I'd be a fool, that's what I'd be. A fool, pure and simple. So I give myself one of those lopsided grins, taking hold of my bellyfat in both hands, wiggling it around to reassure myself about the ludicrous nature of my almost-predicament, thinking how she'd laugh in my face. I start feeling like I've been saved from embarrassment at the eleventh hour and this thought comforts me, sets my mind at ease. There are old men out there who should take a lesson from this, I think to myself with a certain amount of pride. This is self-knowledge. This is what it means to have the strength to face up to the truth, I tell myself, waggling my loose-skinned belly around a bit more for good measure.

I go down into the kitchen, bracing myself for seeing her there, when I hear the sound of clinking pots and someone rummaging around in the icebox, but it's only the Swissman and when I see him I experience an overwhelming surge of disappointment, making me realise I'd secretly been hoping to see her, though fooling myself that I didn't care either way. I make idle conversation with him, all the time keeping one eye on the door, getting more restless by the second as she doesn't appear.

By now it's eight-fifteen. This Swiss guy, I should explain, was my publisher at one time and in fact my friend, too, though many years ago. Since then we've both let our work lapse. He doesn't publish. I don't write. At least, I don't write anything I'd want to see published, nothing I want to send out into the world, defenceless. Thing is, he's clinging to the anxious energy that made him just the man for the job at one time, only now it makes him a pain in the ass. The phrase *lighten up* is constantly in my mind with each word that I say to him, so I start getting nervous that it'll slip out and I make some excuse about checking on my tomato plants and go out the front door to the vegetable patch, cursing under my breath, wishing he'd disappear.

An odd dew seems to have settled in the night and over the remaining tomatoes there's a kind of sheen, a glossy wetness that makes them look all hopeful and rosy, which satisfies me in a strange way, so I stand there admiring them for a few moments, killing time, and then go back to the house, walking cautiously across the grass, trying not to look keen, stopping my legs from breaking into a run just at the thought of her being there in my kitchen. That girl in my kitchen. It seems so unlikely that I start to think I maybe dreamed her up, that the Swissman came alone. Then I have a moment of panic when I reflect that he didn't mention her at all this morning, like she doesn't exist. And in fact this feeling becomes even stronger when I get back inside and she's still not there. I look around wildly, then I see her sun-glasses lying on the kitchen table and feel calmer.

Trying to sound casual, I say to the Swissman, 'You think I should go see if she wants breakfast?' His eyes slide over me, suspicious and snake-like, as though he's suddenly realised what's going on, so when he doesn't reply either way, just carries on rummaging around in the icebox, whistling through his teeth in irritation like a skinny reed blowing in the wind, I don't push it because I can see how he loves her and that he's suddenly realised what his role is going to be this weekend. The jealous would-be lover. Poor bastard, I'm thinking, I wouldn't be the jealous would-be lover of that girl for the world.

But before I have time to think of another way to get her over here, suddenly here she is in front of me. She's wearing some kind of a green cotton dress with little spots on it and buttons all the way up the front. Her shiny red hair is flowing out loose around her shoulders and she doesn't look like she's got any make-up on today, not like last night when she arrived in her smart city clothes. But my, she looks fine. There's no mistaking the simple fact that she's a beautiful young woman, glowing, really glowing with youth and vitality, and I can't help grinning at her like a fool, fussing over her, pouring her coffee, slipping toast in the

Dualit, asking her how she slept, being the perfect host. When I ask her how she slept, she looks at me strangely, like it's a question I should know the answer to. Then she smiles in a funny, embarrassed way, her hair falling across her face as she bends over the toast, buttering away like there's no tomorrow, and says, 'Not too good, actually, even though the bed was comfortable and it was really quiet. But, I don't know, maybe I'm still jet-lagged. I woke up quite early.' Then she casts me another of those strange almost-stares and carries on buttering. When she gives me a look like that I feel like a cheat, because of course I know perfectly well she didn't sleep for at least half of the night, getting up to swim and all the rest, and I think she sees the guilty look in my eyes. So I know I've been found out and start to get resentful again. After all, I was only being courteous.

We go outside to sit around the table on the veranda in the morning sunshine, me at the head in the biggest chair, which is the one I always sit in, her on my left and the Swissman opposite. He says thickly, 'Ah, but she looks charming this morning, no?' looking at her but addressing me. He just can't help himself. She goes pink beneath her freckles when he says this and I feel sorry for her having to fend off all these men panting round her and I'm glad for the second time that day that I've been able to stop myself from making a fool of myself by being one of them. Men can be such pigs, always making women feel like women. So we're munching away at our toast and I'm thinking *What now? Now I've decided I'm not going to get hung up on her, what now? What'll I say to her if I don't tell her she's ruined my life and I want either to kill her or marry her?* I can't fathom out the answer to this question, which is just as well, because otherwise I'd have to do something about it, so I try to stay quiet and make aimless remarks in the right places while the Swissman jabbers on about something or other. I forget what.

At the end of breakfast we've come to a decision. We're going to go into town to buy stuff for lunch. I'm glad of this practical step we're going to take, otherwise I know the strain of being this close together would overwhelm me and I'd not be responsible for my actions. It wouldn't be a pretty sight, I assure you. I'm glad of the diversion of lunch, and I go out to the car to fiddle about with the spark plugs while I wait for them to get ready.

And so I start to swim. Sliding through the wild flood of years without him, tipping over so that the dark surface, unseen, gnaws away at my back as it carries me downstream. The world is a white room above me, and beneath me, always, the fast whisky-stinking river flows on endlessly, boiling and creaking.

There are birds whirling overhead and often the snorts of animals galloping along the river banks or dashing through the shallows at dusk, and the moan of the wind across the surface of the water stretched taut like a young boy's drum-tight chest, blue-skinned and fragile in the bright light.

Sometimes the swollen river, pregnant with vacant rain clouds, crumbles the banks like cheese and the water becomes rusty with ochre soil, an incredible colour. At other times, the chalky land thickens the river like powdered soup heated beyond the boil and fizzing with containment. There are great abandoned stretches too, when the broadening banks loosen their pull on the river's flow and strange eddies and rips claw their way across the calm water, dragging everything beneath the surface as if to preserve the river's design, careless of the land's intention.

There are times, at night, when I feel sharp things at my back, surreptitious stabs that appal me. Blood-cooling touches from out of the depths and then nothing. The heaving river suddenly becomes a vicious riot of hands and all I can do is admire the persistent sky, swallowing back my sickly fear of the unseen things which lurk beneath the skin of the water (perpetual threats which stink unexpectedly). They draw my blood and it is washed away through the days to become a millionth millionth part of the river which flows on beneath the evening sky's gaudy cloak of silence.

Sometimes I hear sounds like angels singing, urging me to sink backwards beneath the lovely surface, to slip down further into the nightless water. There are promises. My spirits soar, imagining an end to solitary disappointment. But promises are evil things and they hover revoltingly along the banks of the river where I can't see them, suspended like poisonous insects with fangs and razor-sharp claws that glint beautifully in the waning summer's dusky afternoons. I believe nothing. Everything is true.

Often the banks of the river are crowded with bawling people. They fall off nonchalantly into the water and are instantly swept away or dragged beneath the surface, waving frantically and unobserved. At other times the lengthening silence floods my watery ears until, abruptly, there is noise again, some scene lurching into earshot around the next curve in the river.

All kinds of things happen on the river bank. The whole of life. Romances, fist-fights, murders, marriages and celebrations, deaths and dances, people fucking and sneering, chomping and idling around without a care in the world while I whiz past or slug past, squinting at everything sideways as the water carries me along, flooding beneath me like the breath of the earth, vital and desperate.

Sometimes, there are things so beautiful beside the river that I have to squeeze my eyes to stop myself sobbing with delight. Young people with hope in their eyes, tearing through the world, courageous, staring wildly at the tiny spinning globe and laughing until they ache, seeing no end to their possibilities and finding light in everything.

I am attentive to all this, right down to the last detail. From famished and hungered-for lovers, to the brief shape of the shadow of the mountains slipping across the surface of the water, all these things affect me with equal force and delicacy as I slide through the tightening noose, stone-hearted. When you've given up hope, everything is of equal importance: all any of it ever amounts to is writing words on a moving river. Still, it carries me along on its efficient, speeding back through the many long years of living without him.

I age. I slide through the decades until I become a better physical match for him, falling into line with who I have always been inside. And unfailingly, above me, stays the white room, the endless turn of the endless pages pale with longing, while behind me, my other life, restless, wildly claws and stamps, jostling for attention, digging its teeth into my skin, as though madly impatient for the sometime order of words which then take up the assiduous reins of motion, swimming up the white paper with nasty ant-marching deliberation, mocking me with their sly prettiness and absolute futility. But what else is there? So I keep swimming downriver, of course I do. The things worth seeing there are more than enough to keep in place the incessant rhythm of idiot hopefulness.

There are times, especially when the river flows through a city, that I think I catch sight of his face, but I am always mistaken. Or at night, sometimes, the rumbling moon swings into view, soaring through the darkness, and I remember another night once, actually dancing at the sight of the moon as though it were a new thing, up to that moment unseen, lurking like fantasy behind the veil of our too-hot imaginations until that precise

moment when we shared eyes like jellied maniacs
and were astonished at our simple recognition. The
river slows right down at moments like this and I
have no desire left even to breathe, so caught up
is my heart in that little act of still-born expectation which still shines, often catching me off
guard. But I always do breathe, the flesh persisting,
merely, as I am swept on and away down the
river, until the moon is out of sight behind the
overhanging trees.

Now her legs are braced against the inside of the car, her slim ankles flexing to take the strain as I drive deliberately too fast round the corners on the way into town. I do this as a test to see what she does. When I shoot her a secretive, below-the-brim-of-my-cap glance to discover what expression she has, there she is, grinning away, looking happy and free as anything which pleases me no end. I'd expected as much from her, not like some girls who act like their mothers, tutting and gritting their teeth melodramatically, or the others who giggle like devious babies. No, she's different and I'm glad of that. But I can't keep my eyes from slipping down her legs, angled out firmly against the floor to stop her from being thrown around too much. She has on some high-heeled shoes now, which she changed into from the sneakers she was wearing at breakfast. I don't question why she changed into them but they make her ankles look pretty so who am I to complain? I also notice that the lowest button on her dress has popped undone, showing off more of those long legs, and I start wondering what Margie in the grocery store will say when she sees her. Probably act all polite and whisper 'Hussy!' under her breath like she was having a genteel sneeze, which thought puts me on the girl's side straight away because, whatever else she is and even though she's ruined my life, she's no hussy, that much is for sure. But I know women. Show me one who isn't jealous of a good-looking woman and I'll find you a man who doesn't care much for breasts. It's just one of those things. Even if he's a fag, he'll have some kind of fascination for breasts, take it from me.

So we're driving along with the Swissman in the back, looking kind of left out, I reckon, like we're a couple in the front and he's our house-guest. I can't help that thought springing into my head, it's there before I can do anything about it. And once it is there I feel suddenly hot and flustered, and I'm sure I must be blushing like some kid having dirty thoughts about his schoolteacher, so I have to fight back an urge to throw her out of the car and be done with it before it gets more out of hand than it already is.

The heat is steady today, radiating down from the sun and back up off the earth with a constancy that only the wild hot wind from the sea can alter, and that only momentarily, gusting through the car windows as we swing around the infrequent, treeless corners. When we pull up in the town outside the liquor store the Swissman jumps out the car, insisting on getting the wine. But this means I'm suddenly left alone with her, the hot midday sun belting down on the dark-blue metal roof of the car, frying us alive like sardines in a can. She takes off her sun-glasses and wipes imaginary sweat off of her forehead, smiling at me, saying, 'Phew, isn't it hot!' in that charming accent of hers. I smile coolly, like the heat doesn't affect me at all, and I make some remark about it always being this way here in the summertime, something like that, while the heavy beads of sweat slither down my spine, hotter each second at the unavoidable sight of her legs disappearing up into her pale green dress and me imagining what kind of panties she must be wearing and what bra (I can tell she's wearing some and that they are both white because of the outline they make against her body, its contours visible through the thin cotton of that little dress).

We don't say anything for a few moments but it is a comfortable silence, like we are getting used to the sensation of sitting together with no one else around, a bit like when a mare is brought to meet her sire before she's going to be covered, an absurd metaphor because I'm no stallion, but I can't help myself thinking like that. It has something to do with the way women are always made to wait, never truly able to rush the swell of time and events in the same way that a man can. But now it's as though I'm on her side, waiting for something to happen too, just like her. Then I say, 'Wonder what's keeping him?' as he still hasn't appeared and she says, 'But it's so beautiful here,' straight away, like she is referring to the fact that he isn't back yet, so meaning the way we are both sitting here together, alone in the midday heat, and something passes between us, some understanding, I swear. She turns to me and smiles again and I know she felt it too, or something like it, doubting of course that she felt anything like the quasi-electric jolt which ricocheted up my spine and through my brain, activating countless little fingers of static pleasure running up and down my legs and arms so I get an almost uncontrollable urge to take a hold of her and grip her tight in my arms like a live wire being put to earth, it seems the only solution. But I stop myself just in the nick of time by leaping out of the car and I praise myself once again for my restraint, by now starting to feel like some kind of medieval knight doing battle against a dragon who each minute threatens to overpower him. Poor bastard that I am.

So I'm jumping around outside the car and she gets out and comes and stands near me, nudging into me briefly – more electric shocks – as she stumbles over some bit of uneven ground and points across the road to the marsh which looks like a perfect field of meadow grass but is no better than a swamp really. Nothing grows there except the grass, even though God knows how many people have tried to make it otherwise. We go across to the other side and take a better look. I have to say I haven't given much thought to the marsh over the years, but she's seeing things in there that I never have, like the way the long-bodied dragonflies flash in the noon sun and the fact that there must be thousands of tiny flowers in among the tough, reedy grass, only you can't see them unless you get up close and peer down from the vantage point of the little bridge, which is where we are when the Swissman comes staggering out of the liquor store with enough bottles of wine and whisky to sink a whole fleet of lushes. He and I start acting like men, talking about the amount we're going to drink later, and she's smirking secretly like she knows the score and will drink us both under the table without any preliminary yakking about it. In fact, this is more or less what she does do, starting with lunch, which we decide to buy ready-made so as we can eat it outside by the pool back home, whenever we get hungry, without any fuss.

Above the city, the sky hangs dark and sullen with menace. The people in the street feel the threat, not sure why it should matter to them if they get wet, but still, feeling that it does matter and they only wish they could do something about it. *It's so unfair*, their vulture-hunched shoulders say, although it baffles them too, the way the raindrops, sliding down their necks to find the naked trail into secrecy, make them squirm with guilty pleasure: an awareness of skin.

I step back out of the flood of people to watch the rainstorm. A girl follows me into the shelter beneath a building. 'Mind if I share your doorway? Oh, God! Always knew I'd die by drowning.' She stands beside me, shivering and chattering her teeth ostentatiously like a child, and I can feel the steam begin to hum from off her skin, trapped beneath her damp coat. 'Oh, hell, will it never stop? I'll be so late.' She chews her fat lower lip, biting off a patch of lipstick and smacking her lips back together again, rubbing them together hurriedly to spread the colour, squinting anxiously at the greenish sky pouring itself towards us as we cower back into the doorway while in the street people hurtle around in confusion. She turns to me and grins weirdly as though noticing me for the first time, comforted, I suppose, by the sight of my tiny middle-aged body, no threat to her, so used to being threatened. 'If we're going to share this doorway so cosily you might as well know my name.' The girl looks back up at the sky, distracted for a moment, then swings back round to look at me, staring hard at my face like a deliberate angel sent to remind me of something. 'Lucille,' she says, 'I'm Lucille,' and I remember where I heard that name before, although it was many years ago now: one of his wives.

By the time she's finished confessing, 'In fact, I'm not late for anything,' we're in one of the few bars I know of where you can get a drink at 10 a.m. and she's telling me her life history, which is sad and well-rehearsed. She's looking at me strangely the whole time she tells it, cocking her head at me like a coy lap-dog, twitching her ears and batting her lashes, and I can't fathom out why she's bothering with this charade, because what we do next is merely inevitable, just as it's inevitable that she'd be called Lucille. But I love to watch her putting on this little show for me. It's perfectly charming. And I can see how much pleasure it gives her. It's also her way of staving off the disappointment we're bound to feel, both knowing that we're not *the ones* and admitting it at such an early stage. So I'm flattered and saddened by the way she acts out all the rules of this crazy game we're playing and I wonder whether *he* was similarly flattered and whether that was why he married her, the other Lucille, happy to believe her cooings and quick, pink cheeks.

In the bar, like abandoned kings, stubborn old men hunch in the corners, guarding their drinks, trying to blend into the stench of pissy beer and sore-looking flocked wallpaper. Watching these men disappear and be replaced is my guarantee of seeing time pass. The girl Lucille is giggling violently now, humping her pneumatic shoulders up and down so that the slippery drink in front of her leaps and slops inside the glass, flecking the table with bright beads of gold. I eye her suspiciously, finding her laughter appalling, bored to tears by her *and then he saids*, not wanting to see her go, wishing I could find some way of keeping her around now that I've found her. She's crying, though, not laughing as I'd imagined, and her steady stream of tears dripping on to the table matches the plunging rain beyond the window. The old men's eyes flicker across us, noticing nothing, taking everything in disinterestedly, all things become equal for them now that their lives have been squashed by alcohol, levelled out into king-doms of indeterminate value and excitement.

By the time her sobs have subsided she has her grubby little fingers inside my shirt, fumbling around like a boy at a school dance, inept and thrilling. I want to find a way to draw the situation out for as long as possible so I take her up on her insincere question, big-eyed and cheaply faked innocence shining out of her moonlike face. I tell her how it began, how I met him, the whole thing. The blankness radiating hotly from her eyes is exhilarating and I feel as though I'm diving sky-wards into a pool of black hope, leaping crazily into her lovely empty eyes, as bored to distraction as my eyes must have looked to her just a minute ago.

As I tell her the story I feel the change within me. This is my way of being able to see him again. Also a way to escape him, if momentarily. It never fails. And even now, sitting here with the lovely Lucille, I see that he has taken my place beside her and her hands are upon *him* now, not me, snaking their way inside his shirt, twisting around his neck, drawing his head down towards her. He's pulling away slightly, just enough to keep telling her his story, which isn't a way of telling her about himself at all but rather of making clear just what he wants from her, what she should expect to do for him, demanding her compliance, asserting his expectations like a foot in the door. It seems as though she understands because she's trembling with desire for him now, almost shimmering with the bright glow of lust, her limpid eyes widening at the curving desolation of his stories, blinking in a silent *yes* as he pulls out every last tooth of resistance from her, so fast that she doesn't notice the flood of her life leaving her like a broad hand lifted off the mouth of memory, telling him everything.

Oh Lucille. Her hands are all over him now, gladly relinquishing her life's burden of *but I couldn'ts* and *if only he hads* to their fierce embrace, rushing her tongue across him. Then he pulls her towards him as though trying to stagger to his feet but dragging her against him instead and lifting up one of her legs so that she's sitting astride him, her legs wrapped about him, almost cracking with the strain of gripping tightly around his thick waist, screwing herself down on to him as though she wants to burn right through him. But he holds her, delicately, lifting her lightly off him to watch her wildly seething lust held in suspense until he's seen enough and he lets her go, falling back against the sweating, cushioned wall of the bar, and she slips off him, breathing hard, slumping beside him like a lump of dead meat, and he can see himself clearly again. The vision disgusts him and is more disappointing even than he remembers it. He throws some money on to the table in front of her – *Don't worry, you'll forget about me soon enough* – and strolls out of the bar into the street, whistling tunelessly, not even hearing the sobs which belch violently out of her sated body, now bloodless and full of hope.

~

I sit with my back to the west side of the house trying to decide whether I'll go for a swim before lunch, squinting up at the lowering sky which looks like it's preparing itself for a storm, when suddenly there she is again, coming out of the house over on the far side, real slow, like she hasn't seen me yet. She's wearing a white bikini with some kind of black leopard spots on it, is what it looks like, and I stop breathing as I watch her coming out into the day, walking out of my house, and I feel a strange surge of pride that it's *my* house that this graceful little creature is coming out of. She looks up at the sky and smiles, seeing the rain clouds gathering over in the east, then she sees me and waves from across the water, shouting, 'Looks like rain,' and the second that she says this, as though on cue, the clouds rumble and roar, and great drops of water come pouring out, all at once, no build-up or anything, just like a tropical rain-storm, sudden and crazy.

The Swissman has sneaked up behind me and is muttering something about how he thinks the weather is rotten and without reason, but my eyes

103

are glued on her while she's grinning like a surprised little cat, grinning at me and at the sky both, before spinning round once and leaping into the pool any old how with a howl of delight. She goes under the surface, then swims across towards where I am, shouting, 'It's wonderful, come on! Come on!' like these are the last days and everything depends on it. 'It's my favourite thing in the world, to swim in the rain like this!' she's yelling at me like a mad thing, bobbing around in the water, and I remember how earlier that day she'd said that something else was her favourite thing in all the world, I think it was the colour of the sky above the marshy green grass, and I reflect that she's the kind of person who has many favourite things, one of those people who love a lot, which makes me feel lucky and jealous all at once.

The Swissman is still scowling away behind me. Even though I haven't taken my eyes off her for a minute I can tell that's what he's doing, feel his discomfort grinding into my back, and I get an urge to smash his stupid Swiss face in there and then, and be done with it. But of course I don't because he's my guest and my friend, too, after all, so I just ignore him and am happy when I hear the mosquito metal mesh door swing closed as he goes back inside to brood. She's swimming around singing now, just tuneless la la las but a lunatic sound which makes me laugh. 'Come on! Quick, quick, before the rain stops!' she starts yelling, so I hare off inside to go change into my swimming trunks, which I do at the speed of light, then, feeling foolishly over-hasty, I slow up as I come down the stairs so as she doesn't think I'm too eager. I avoid looking in the mirror. I figure, why torment myself?

She's still la la la-ing when I get outside and looks happier still when she sees me, which makes me feel reckless and just like her, so I leap into the pool as she did, thrashing around, splashing and raising hell, which makes her laugh even harder, pulling faces, yelling 'Yahoo!' like a wild thing. Then the Swissman comes out again, fully dressed, scowling at us and pretending it's a smile. But there's no mistaking it's a scowl all right and he looks mighty pissed, but what the hell, this is fun! I'm thinking. I might be old, but this is fun!

Instead of letting up, the rain gets louder and harder, and it seems to drive her crazier the more it pelts down. There's thunder, too, and great shattering cracks of lightning, breaking the sky in two with perfect white light above the dark rim of the forest. For a little moment then she wears an afraid expression as a lightning bolt really looks like it might set fire to the pool it seems so close, and she swims slower, closer to me, asking in a nervous voice now, 'Is it normally this loud?' and I feel all big and strong like I could protect her, so I tell her, 'Oh, sure, it's always like this here, you just got to expect it.' She looks a bit uncertain, but when I suggest we get out of the pool and go get us some lunch I don't notice her complaining. We get out and I have my towel ready by the edge so I hand it to her, holding it out for her to walk into like a little child might walk into the outstretched towel held in the arms of its mother, which makes me feel even more big and protective; it feels right somehow.

The Swissman looks really pissed now and turns quickly, going back inside, muttering about getting the wine. She goes off to her room and I go take a shower before lunch.

I see him ever more clearly now as he stumbles outside, glancing up quickly at the blackening sky before setting off alone into the city, swinging along into the dusk beneath the fizzing street lights and weaving easily among the tottering people *cluttering up the streets* is, I know, how he thinks of them, all of them seeming the same to him, all incomprehensible and repellent. 'There are days', he admitted to me through grinding teeth, shame-faced with terror and looking away, 'when it eats me up, this hatred and fear of crowds.' Most of the time he pretends he likes them. And if someone were to ask him how he sees himself, he'd say: Equally at home in a crowd or alone. But it would be a lie and he'd smile as he said it, challenging disbelief.

If it were possible, he told me, though not in these words, he'd rid the whole world of crowds and keep only two things: fucking, as the only human contact, an abstract thing that happens without the disgusting afterbirth of post-coital humiliation, something that keeps only the fore-runners of pleasure, the almost-touches, the slight glances and all the long seconds of anticipation; and writing, as a desperate reminder of the sorrow running wildly along the crust of the earth.

So now I watch him, knowing how the scene will unfold, while he walks through the jumbling people as though possessed. His eyes swim with a delirious hunger and his large hands are tightened into two weapons, concealed nervously in the pockets of his overcoat. The night darkens and thickens. There is a queasy mist settling all across the square and things lurk in the warm beneath car engines, hiccuping on the brackish fumes. He plunges on through the night, glinting angrily as lovers in the street paw one another obscenely and laugh ostentatiously as if they were naked and alone. He crashes into a woman who reminds him of his mother and he winces, hurrying past, expecting the thwack of the outstretched palm, the denigration of his secret thoughts, her ability to expose him to scorn with one twitch of her lips and a single word like a well-placed lever, toppling his private world into foolishness.

There are people for sale everywhere, though they would deny their price. A cat-like girl rubs herself against him as he passes an alleyway, drawing him into the narrow space between two high buildings: a women's hospital and a restaurant where smartly dressed people troop in and out in stiff-backed file, checking their watches. He gives her some money and she draws blood on his neck with one neat nip of her teeth, so he pummels her hard against the wall, making her yelp like a damaged animal, pitifully, until she becomes subdued. He notices her fragile smile of triumph and he feels ashamed, fearful of her, watching her beat him, powerless to stop her from humiliating him as he pins her elegant neck against the bricks, trying to look away, anywhere but into those blue, triumphant eyes, hating him so casually. He feels better on his knees, slipped down into the puddle of piss and rainwater which gurgles into the drain which her worn-heeled feet straddle. Her 'Go on then, you filthy bugger' is better than nothing and when she bucks against his mouth he feels a certain loosening of the noose around his neck, something close to absolution, at least for now, until at last her piggish grunts and hair-tearing antics collapse and fall from her and she sags, clinging briefly to him – 'You aren't half bad, mate' – before slouching off to set up her vigil at the gaping mouth of the alleyway as before, forgetting him already as he passes by her and walks away into the night.

~

After I've got everything ready for lunch I sit on the veranda with the Swissman, cracking into the first bottle of the day, trying not to stare too hard at the door to the house which I gauge she'll be coming out of any minute now. The Swissman catches me glancing behind him at the door and gives me a weaselly look as much as to say: *Don't even think about it, you miserable fuck.* So I fix him with a hard stare as if to say: *I'll do what the hell I want, just watch me.* And then there's an awkward almost-moment between us, like there is between animals who get hungry for the same bit of meat. But then while we're doing that macho shit, there she is coming out of the house and straight away I stop thinking about any of that, because as she starts walking towards me she looks up at the sky which is now bright-washed blue with not a cloud in sight as though the rain has cleared it all away, and above her, arching right across the dark trees, there is the most perfect rainbow I've ever seen, a complete arch of solid colour from one end to the other. I can't believe I didn't notice it before now, then I realise that it's just one of so many things I never noticed before she came here and I sit for a moment lost in the appreciation of this idea, much in the same way you sit for a second looking at a present someone gives you that you love but never realised before then that you would value such a thing, struck by the curious novelty of it all.

'Look!' she says softly so as I can only just catch her words, which don't seem to be meant for either me or the Swissman but more for herself, to mark the occasion of seeing the rainbow for her own private remembering. When she sits down opposite me at the table, smiling with her whole body like only really happy people are able to, she says, 'Rainbows are my favourite things in all the world,' and I laugh out loud, reminding her that she's already said that about a number of other things and they can't all be favourites, now can they? and she looks down at her plate, playing with her food a bit. I can tell that she's blushing, which makes her look even prettier though uncomfortable, so I don't push that any further and pour her out a glass of wine, making a toast: 'To the weekend!'

She looks up from staring at her plate, her face suddenly gone a little pale, and raises her glass to chink it against the Swissman's first, then mine. He guzzles down his wine in one slurp and I reflect that it's a load of bull when people say the Swiss are civilised, especially if this one is anything to go by. Then when she chinks glasses with me her face looks sad about the eyes and there's a tightness around her mouth which I don't understand. She looks a bit like she did when the thunder was blasting overhead of us in the pool earlier and I get the same urge to protect her from whatever it is that's making her that way, but what can I do with that man here as well? I'm filled with a sudden feeling of irritation towards him, which is quickly followed by a surge of gratitude that he brought her here in the first place, then both of those feelings jostle around in my mind next to the thought that there's something wildly inappropriate about him being here with us at all, that he might as well just leave, fuck off back to Switzerland or wherever the hell he wants to, which he couldn't do fast enough as far as I'm concerned, and finally I'm gripped by the shock of having been thinking any of these things in the first place and I get up and go inside suddenly on some pretext, avoiding looking at her as I go.

Inside the kitchen the air is cool and there's not much light on account of the dark-blue blinds I keep up at the windows with this express purpose in mind. When I get inside I head straight to the drinks cupboard and take a pull on the bottle of vodka I keep handy, not risking smelling of alcohol by swigging the whisky, which I'd actually prefer, but that's not important right now, I'm thinking, I just need to get my mind back to normal and stop it from having such wild ideas about this girl. It's all she is! I tell myself. Just a girl! She's young enough to be my granddaughter is the God's honest truth, which is so bald, put like that, that I almost break into a grin, but it's the kind of grin that feels more like a savage baring of teeth I'm so angry at the order of things. Her age and my fast-approaching death start to seem now like an obscene combination of circumstance when pitted against this pure sensation of something close to innocence, is the only way I can think of to describe it, it feels so straightforwardly truthful and merely unavoidable now. I'm grinding my teeth together so hard it feels like they'll start to splinter any minute and my jaw twinges like it too wants to remind me of my decrepitude. *What the hell am I going to do?* is all I can think, getting more pissed and mean by the second, so I take another good hard pull on the vodka, then start getting fixed on the thought that I want to race outside, kill the lousy Swissman with my bare teeth and storm back through time, taking the girl with me, tearing along backwards, destroying every-thing I've done without her, all that wasted time before I met her, none of which matters now. It's not the impossibility of the future, which will have to be without her, I tell myself, don't go thinking otherwise, no, it's not the empty, hopeless, moreover *brief* future which bothers me, not one bit, the future can go hang itself now for all I care and I'll be dead soon anyway, so what the hell, it's not that at all, it's all the backward years, seventy-five years behind me which were all a waste because they were all without her. Empty. An empty life which up until precisely eight-fourteen yesterday evening I was proud of in a kind of way, and, if not proud, certainly making like I was and, if not making like I was, certainly feeling kind of contented if not actually happy most of the time, and what it all comes down to is that until now I've never understood what it could actually mean to be alone. Not merely lonely, but absolutely alone in the universe, because that's what happens when you meet the one person in the whole of creation who is *just like yourself*, the only one who can even potentially relieve your loneliness.

And there she is, I think, the panic now turned into a calm, dreadful fear, way beyond anger or anxiety, just a dreadful fear that won't shift, however hard I try to get it off my back, there she is, sitting on my lousy veranda cool as you please and unawares, too, and I have to stop myself crumpling up on to the floor and laughing my head off I'm so afraid at what this means. Some people have tried to fix this feeling with a little four-letter word which is pathetically inappropriate to the way I'm feeling now, which is a completely new feeling, one I've never even gotten a sniff at before, old as I am; it's as though I've been ground up in a meat-grinder, painted a different colour, spat out into a strange place without protection and the only name I've got to put to it is FEAR, which I think about in big letters because even that word doesn't get close to it, so I give up trying to find a word that does and close my eyes for a minute, letting the dark-blue light spread calm across my face before going slowly outside, smiling at the Swissman like everything is dandy, but avoiding looking at her as though my life depends on it, which in a way it does.

'More wine?' I say, waving around the bottle I had the forethought to bring out from the kitchen.

Of course, in my mind's eye, I can see that what he doesn't notice is the way the girl raises her chin in vindication as he shoulders his way past her and on through the dirty night. But I know he feels it. He suspects her eyes, too, pressed against his back like a clawed caress, marking his skin. But she does not watch him and he rounds the corner of the street unobserved, certain only that he has lost something, given up on one more thing, and he's bereft in the face of the thought: *How can I ever get it back*? It's what makes him hungry and he can't stop the chomp of his teeth, gnashing angrily until they almost splinter with smashing against themselves. I follow him, wondering how things will transpire this time, admiring the broad hunch of his back slinking away into the gloom, leading me on.

He wheels round the corner and clings to the iron railings momentarily, staring at the star-filled sky, gazing wolf-like at the full moon as though he has never seen it before, gasping as if out of breath with wonder before heaving his big frame up a short flight of iron steps on the outside of a squat

116

building. The black door opens into a short, yellowing hallway. Off it, at the far end, there is a curtain of bright multicoloured plastic leading to the bar. I clang after him up the iron stairway and go to sit opposite him on the far side of the room. He turns to me and grunts, unsmiling, as though he'd expected to see me here.

Apart from the two of us and the uninterested barman, the place is empty. The window has been roughly painted over with black paint and through the cracks the street sheds a tranquil gloss of idly flickering colours into the room, otherwise lit only by a strip of gaudy Chartreuse-green neon running along the length of the bar beneath the upturned bottles. I wait for him and watch. As though caught between deep sleep and nervous, alert wakefulness, he alternately slumps and shakes himself upright, twitching in my direction as though I have him caught on an electric wire and am hauling him in with a gradual but deliberate cruelty that makes him wince. When he looks at me, his black eyes boring into me through the watery light, it's as if he's trying to catch sight of me through a crowd of people. His eyes dart to and fro, losing and then seeing me as if I were dodging jostling bodies in his line of sight. When he comes across to sit beside me, there's an anger in the way he sits down that is more like defeat

117

and his bundled hands clench against themselves as though they were squeezing out the blood from his brain, trying desperately to quieten it.

He fills the room. There is nothing else but him, surrounded by light and a tiny veil of heat shrouding his big body so that fragments of him are always touching something, touching me indiscriminately. By the time he's let go of my head, held quickly and hard between his meatish palms to assert that it is not his own, that it is a different shape, weight and texture, something has started to change inside him. His skin is racing with this new expectation and an ambivalent fear of certainty, knowing the goal. I watch the change in him, feeling it catch hold in me too, running hot-footed through me, contagious like fire, feeling the spiders start to crawl across my scalp and the gnawing groan begin to swell in my jumping veins, leaping now like boiling steel until the cool of his fingertips dawdling inside the gaps between my knuckles soothes me like nothing else and I wait, calmed momentarily like an animal that has been covered with a black cloth before the final gunshot.

Later that night when the stars have already begun to fade, lit up by the sunlight creeping towards the city from the other side of the world, we walk together through the deserted streets like ancient lifelong lovers. Our slow pace and simple, deliberate proximity is a vow, and when we climb the railings into the park to lie stretched out together beneath the crowded Scots pines I'm stung by the hot weight of time dancing out before us so that I cling to him, dazzled by the possibility of a life spent alongside each other, seeing it again as if for the first time.

The sap drips from the damp pines. Infrequent traffic sounds define the distant city. It feels as though the whole world has conspired in these few moments, wiping clean everything that has happened before now and breaking down the doors of secrecy which cover the future. Uncourageous, soft-limbed with sleep, we try to prolong the brink of disbelief in vain, finding pleasure as children might: the simple exultation of familiarity. But seeing that rim of darkness together is all that has ever really mattered and all that there could have been between us, in whatever circumstance we might have met. The whole of life summed up in one last look at the wild untrammelled *yes* which collapses, even as it happens, into the treacherous ebb of time like a perfect island lost for ever beneath the ocean.

Perhaps that is how it would have been between us, had we in fact met like this, I think to myself, seeing the entire scene unravel before me, enjoying each moment of luxurious memory as I wait for the longed-for events to run their course once more. So now I stand up, scattering pine needles about me as I turn from him and start to walk away across the wet grass and on towards the morning which is humming now with chance and endless variation.

~

I get through lunch by being courteous and not looking at her, simply avoiding looking at her, which isn't easy on account of the fact that she's sitting directly opposite me. I get a crick in my neck with the effort but I figure that's a small price to pay. The Swissman is in overdrive anyway, burbling on about something or other, which releases me from a host's pressure of having to lead conversation. There are a few sticky moments, like when she lights up a cigarette after we've finished eating, although she explained that she doesn't smoke as a rule, and I get the urge to have one too, although I gave up over thirty years ago. I think, *What the hell? What is there to lose now anyway?* So I say recklessly, 'I think I'll have one of those.' But before I get a chance to light one up myself she's offering me the packet, flicking the Swissman's silver lighter for me.

Now there's a little wind picked up, skimming through the trees at us, so I have to cup my hands around the cigarette so as it doesn't go out and as I do this I accidentally brush her hand, which gives me a jolt like someone's hit me on the back with a bare electric cable – this being only the fourth time I've touched her. Her hand seems to be shaking like she can't hold the lighter still, so I take hold of her wrist, real gentle, to get a light off of her. What else could I do? I can't help but catch her eyes and she looks down, flustered and blushing sweetly so that her freckled skin is as red-rosy as her hair, and I want to draw her towards me then and kiss her lovely mouth. But of course I don't because of the Swissman who is starting sincerely to aggravate me again, just when I'd been trying real hard not to let him get to me. So I let her hand go and then press the hand that touched her against my thigh under the table where she can't see it, squeezing it up against my skin like a tattoo, *the closest I'll ever get to her*, I remind myself, *so don't even start to think otherwise, be happy with this and no more*, although I know by now that that's a lie and I'll never be satisfied whatever happens.

So there I am, trying to concentrate on the Swissman, not her, and all of a sudden she says, 'You're both going to have to excuse me. I'm just going to go and do a bit of work on a story I'm writing. You don't mind, do you?' And I could kick myself. This wasn't the plan at all. I didn't want to make her go off like that, but I reckon I was paying too much attention to him because she says this in a small voice, though trying to sound nonchalant and polite. I can tell she's hurt, which puzzles me. The Swissman raises the half-drunk bottle of wine at her, dangling it from his scrawny arms, swilling the wine around as much as to say *Don't worry, baby, we're men together, we're happier drinking without you anyway* – which makes me want to smash the bottle over his lousy Swiss head and be done with it. So I look at her in a way that I hope is imploring but not openly disrespectful to the Swissman and try to will her not to go, but she isn't looking at me anyway and goes right on and leaves, almost running back to her room to get her stuff, like she couldn't get out of there quick enough.

I pour the Swissman an extra large tumbler of wine in the hope it'll shut him up, but he keeps blabbing on like we're the best of friends, which I suppose we almost were until he brought her here. I try not to look over his shoulder to watch her settling down to work, over beneath the shade of one of the largest pines, with its low branches sticking out at right angles to the reddish trunk. Her back is turned to us and her head covered by a large straw hat, so I can't see her face at all, only her hand moving around over the pages of her book, sure and confident, just like I once was myself, which reminds me of the many long hours

123

spent underneath that very same tree over the years, enraptured in a posture much the same as hers, until, of course, one particular day in June exactly ten years ago this month, the weather and temperature rather like today, I suppose, when I went outside in the bright light of early morning, the clear light almost luminous as it bounced up into the sky off the vast waters of the ocean, to find my son hanging from the lowest branch of the Scots pine. Perfectly still, his skinny arms and legs looked almost elegant, as though gorgeously attenuated by that posture where at last he didn't slouch as was his way when he stood usually, which made his mother mad at him, telling him he'd never be able to stand up for himself in life if he couldn't even stand up straight and now his lolling head also absolutely immobile because there was no breeze that morning. So, rooted to the spot, staring, I expect as though appearing to be seeing for the first time the effects of some until then almost unbelieved experiment, and in the near-silence, I remember cocking my ear as though I might still hear the rumble of the previous night's argument. His mother's 'You have no heart!' Some story I'd written that had aggravated her. She saw herself in it, was outraged at the similarity of the other family on the page, the one with the slouching son, embittered wife, uneasy, disappointed husband. 'You cannot care for us,' she accused, 'just to twist us into stories like this.'

Meanwhile as we yelled like pigs, from behind the door the sound of the boy's escaping footsteps was the only thing that stopped me strangling her complaining neck. She had reason to be angry: I was never so happy that I didn't seek to test what joy I had with mockery, attempt to spoil it with insults. In this way I had ruined all my happiness, despising its fearful fragility. Then I called my fear cleverness, even wisdom, but it was never more than an attachment to restlessness so strong it had become mere brutality, the most cringing sort of fear. That morning was my proof. Well, I haven't published anything since then. There hasn't ever seemed to be much sense in it.

Even as I dream I am certain of one thing: if I don't walk away at that precise moment I will have to kill him. My hands upon his neck. The quick slip of the sharpened blade across his childishly soft wrists, slicing the pounding veins until they slacken and at last become silent. I know that at this instant his surprise will be merely casual, disinterested. There will be a bright glow of relief playing around his smooth brows. Birds singing, trees swaying in the breeze from off the lake, the whole scene in immaculate collusion. So of course I don't turn round but stroll off until I'm swallowed up again by the city and the morning carries on as before, barely a wrinkle across the placid surface of things.

But however far and fast I walk, the thought of killing him will not loosen its velvet grip from off my mind. Behind my eyes the flames of thick intent lick upwards into the stiffening veins feeding my brain so that I can think of nothing else but how to kill him, imagine nothing else but the surge of flames chewing up his skin like a thousand mouths gnawing all at once. Teeth everywhere. The stench

126

of burning meat. His dear sweet face slipping away from his too-fragile bones, the soft skin melting weirdly into the flames. His hair frazzled like nylon. His eyeballs dissolving like jelly dropped into a pan of boiling water and the whole thing happening in silence, because it is the sound of his restless breathing and his certain screams that I couldn't bear.

I walk away. But now as I walk I stumble towards the edge of sleeplessness. Beyond my window, the flames from the sun are fingering the eyes of the city open one by one, sticking their fingertips beneath the lids of the buildings to wake each one up in a swathe of beautiful light until the whole city is doused with hot fire as the sun sways overhead, dizzying the people in the streets who all turn to stare, pointing upwards, smiling at the autumn sun beaming down on to them from the cloudless blue sky.

Waking from sleep that morning I remember this dream with the same curious dread as always. I turn over in bed to face the window, putting my back to my husband, still sleeping soundly beside me, the curve of his old back a reproach against my screaming mind which has defeated me again, even in sleep. So much time has passed without any possibility of this dream ever having been a reality that it baffles me to think of it. So many long years now, when before, *then*, each tiny second held a lifetime of chance in it. The disproportionate weight of events to time is a cruel violence against hope. That two days could light up a whole life appals me: so much else of various worth and kindness has been forgotten. Even each present moment shrinks into oblivion, always shrinking and diminishing to nothing, while that one brief time of what? of love? spreads itself over my naked eyes, covering over the whole world as I look out across it into another morning, all yearning reduced to one barren thought: perhaps *now* I've killed him, perhaps *now, today*, I can walk away from him for ever while he lies there and burns, helpless, on the putrid earth; perhaps *now* I can carry on with the rest of my life without his dogged eyes upon me, without his prying, soft-tipped fingers against my throat, squeezing just enough against my bare skin to jolt me like lightning into the present, filling me up with himself as my eyes blink tight shut to banish the world's filthy caress just for one instant of vivid and profound calm. It's all I have left: revisiting that single, bleak moment's fierce hiatus, which I wouldn't change, not for anything.

The day stretches out into afternoon and I find a certain happiness just to be near where she is. Even if it is at a distance of a hundred yards further than I'd like it to be, at least I can look at her, watch her writing away beneath the massive pine trees, her tiny figure fragile-seeming among the lengthening shadows. Then all of a sudden she leaps up and chucks her pen down with a flourish of triumph, spinning round to see if we're still there, I guess, and seeing us sitting beneath the shade of the veranda, hard at work on a bottle of whisky, she waves wildly at us and comes bounding over, leaving her writing things beneath the tree. 'What now? Will you take us to see the sea?' she asks me, smiling in an ecstatic, exhausted way like she's just run a marathon. The Swissman, dazed and limp like a wind-torn willow tree (I've been filling his glass as fast as was decent in the secret hope of knocking him out cold), somehow picks up on the word 'beach' and starts saying 'The beach! The beach!' like it's all he's ever wanted. She's grinning at me, looking from me to him like she can read my mind so as I almost blush with imagining what she would think if she actually knew the lewd and hopeless nature of my thoughts concerning her and how I've been trying to get the Swissman drunk enough just to fall out of the picture altogether. So I get up too quickly and lead the way round the house to the car and we set off for the beach as the afternoon draws itself out deliciously across the fields and forests which border the road leading from my house down to the sea.

The tide is out, and between the dunes along the shoreline and the edge of the ocean itself there is a long slick of ankle-deep water, warmed by the sun. It's at this point that the Swissman gives up walking along beside the girl and me. He suddenly sits down on his jacket on the sand, unfolding his long-limbed body and stretching flat out with his hands behind his head, looking for all the world like a weary sea creature stranded at low tide. I could have jumped for joy at this chance, unexpectedly given to me to be alone with her, but I act as nonchalant as I'm able to in the circumstances and we continue our walk along the beach, leaving him to fall asleep in the fading sunlight or get swept away by the tide for all I care.

We walk together, moving closer to where the shallow sea curls over the wet sand, smoothing out the rippled surface of the ocean bed, disguising rocks and shells with a soft film of fine mud. We've both taken off our shoes already and so we walk along looking down at the prints our feet make which are instantly swallowed up by the sea, filled with water and obliterated. There is no one else about. The Swissman is the only living person within sight and becoming ever more distant, and this fact, coupled with the vastness of the scene, makes our situation seem suddenly intimate. I'm acutely aware of her proximity, her bare legs beside mine as we walk along side by side, like a regular couple is how it seems. I can't stop myself having that thought as a sensation of pure contentment takes a hold of me, warming me up deep in my heart. Just this, nothing else; it's all I ask for, nothing more than this. Then, out of the blue, she takes my hand, like it's the most natural thing in all the world for us to be doing, walking together along the beach, hand in hand like lovers.

Her hand is warm and soft, just as I'd expected, but surprising in its strength, too, when her fingers press between mine, moving between the base of my fingers slowly as though to find a more comfortable place, yet never ceasing to move, minutely, as two bodies might, caught in a fiercely tender, struggling embrace. I can't bear to turn to

131

look at her because I know that then I'll have to kiss her, which will ruin everything and she'll let go of my hand and have an expression of surprise and confusion – or disgust even – on her face which I couldn't ever bear to see. So I just point out to sea with my other hand and make some irrelevant remark about a boat or something on the horizon, neither of us breaking our stride, keeping an even pace, nice and easy along the beach. Inside, I'm boiling with desire and a kind of pride, is how it feels, something akin to admiration for the sweetness of this lovely creature, wanting her in a way that transforms my idea of what it means to want something, realising that what I'd previously called want must've been some kind of dim animal instinct, ordinary and straightforwardly satisfied, even vulgar. Now want has become something marvellous and shocking, bringing with it whole new worlds of excitement and fire, endless visions and promises of happiness.

Then, too soon, we're walking an arc back towards the dunes and round towards the Swissman's prone shape, a low ridge barely rising above the soft curves of the beach. And I realise in a surprisingly calm way and with perfect certainty that I have never in my life been happier than at this moment, here, with her, like this,

taking a walk along the beach in the fading sunlight of late afternoon.

So each day I try a new method of murder. I have done this all the long years of my life, ever since meeting him. I remember how it began: walking towards him up the curve of the driveway. It was early evening. He stopped dead still, a look of panic to match my own upon his face as he stared at me as though lost for words. By the time he regained his composure I had passed him and gone on up into the house, all the time cursing wildly to myself, thinking *Now what am I going to do? Now what?*

As soon as I saw him that day I knew I'd have to find a way to destroy him, scrub him out of my mind before he festered and grew like a cancer, impossible to shift and fatal. It seemed easy enough at first. After all, he was an old man and, moreover, an old man stumbling on the brink of a predicted death. He'd had four wives and God only knows how many other women. I realised I'd have to be vigilant. *I can play at this game, too*, I thought in triumph, momentarily convinced, watching him slyly, waiting for him to betray himself. But all I saw was a confusion to match my own and a frank fascination that made my skin burn whenever he caught me staring at him with the same curious surprise mixed up with blatant lust which was written across my face, as unmistakable as a banner.

That same night I set to work, plotting his downfall. It was easy. When I'd finished, I slept soundly, full of gratitude. I'd given him a new life, is all, written him into a story and merely watched what happened, unflinchingly watched him until he was no more than words, a series of pleasant phrases strung together into a self-defeating loop of harmless charm. By the time I finished it was almost morning but I was so filled up with gladness and relief that I didn't miss sleep and leapt out into the new day feeling invincible and then straight away foolish the moment I saw him.

No, he wasn't dead, not yet. I hadn't noticed the way his wrists, strong and broad with working in the garden each day, had an incredible elegance about their movements when put to delicate tasks like handing me a glass of wine, passing me a cigarette, lightly turning the pages of a book. I hadn't yet written down the way his breath snagged in his throat when he caught me watching him from beneath the brim of my hat, squinting against the bright sunlight flooding the garden at midday, brightening up the dusty, motionless air

135

beneath the tall Scots pines so that it became fragile, glittering strangely. Nor had I given enough thought to the way he said my name, rubbing the word across his lips as though tasting it and famished for more, curious at the unfamiliar sound, trying to imprint himself upon the word so that now it is as though the name is no longer my own but belongs to him. 'Have it! Take it, please!' I wanted to implore him, hearing him turn the sound around inside his throat before handing it back to me politely, the word now changed beyond recognition, leaving me with no further use for it.

That afternoon I tried again, writing him into another story so that I could watch him more attentively, take a closer look and see those things about him that would, certainly, be a disappointment. It was hard. I sweated and trembled with the effort of it and thought, in finishing, that I'd almost done it, almost, but I'd need one more thing, just a gesture, an indication of some blindness or blankness from him, anything to destroy my suspicion that we had, by some miraculous chance and despite the fifty-five years, the lifetime, separating us, slipped together on to the same crest of time, even if just for a moment, and were looking about us at the world with new, shared eyes. But there was nothing and his hand covering mine was a confirmation: he felt it too.

Later that night, with his body deep inside me, pounding out our last breaths in terrible unison, I saw the darkness looming beyond those present moments and I was scared out of my wits, unable to stop the racing of my mind as it aged instantly, becoming a sharp point of shivering clarity, showing me my future, emptied of him completely, more bleak and certain and hounded by chaos than I'd ever anticipated.

I crept back to my room just as the dark rooks leapt wildly into the dawn sky, flapping their grotesque wings across the incandescent blue as it gradually flooded with colour from the east. The empty bed was cold. I lay beneath the stiff blankets, stretching my body out across the narrow bed, lying there dead still, rigid like an obelisk, listening to the sounds of morning with serene detachment.

~

Although it must sound crazy to some people, that hand-holding incident on the beach brought me to such a pitch of excitement – that such a thing was possible! – that the next few hours when we did simple things like buy stuff for dinner from the store at the beach, just ordinary things happening real fast and sweet, I was somehow borne along by the sheer pleasure I'd felt when she held my hand, and before I knew it we were back at the house, unpacking the groceries in the kitchen. Being there slowed things down again for some reason, it's hard to explain. I think it had something to do with the mingling of likelihood and unlikelihood of her touching me again, so I felt suddenly heavy, stubborn, unable to affect her decision or whatever the fates might decide for me.

So here we are, unpacking the bags, and the Swissman, unusually silent and pale-looking, mutters something about thinking he'll just take a short nap and off he goes, leaving us alone together for the second time that day. *What luck*! I think, feeling instantly better now that I've got her to myself. So I fix her a drink, one of my famous whisky sours, then put the wine in the icebox to chill. We get busy like our lives depend on it, fussing around together in the kitchen with her making a real mess when she gets to cooking, throwing things about, forgetting where she's put stuff, mixing everything up until it's a miracle anything gets done at all. But it makes me laugh and she laughs along with me, even though the joke's on her, which is a good characteristic to possess I've always thought. She's flinging stuff around the kitchen with such abandon I figure she'll need an apron and I get her one which reads 'If you can't stand the heat, get your butt off the stove', which I've always found kind of lame as a joke, but suddenly it seems funny and we're both roaring with laughter as I put the apron over her head, giving me a chance to touch her lovely red hair as I lift it out of the way before fixing up the ties around her waist. This seems to please her as she goes quiet and half turns her head as I'm doing this, saying in a soft voice, her face only about ten inches from mine, 'Thank you, that's very charming of you,' which makes me feel real chivalrous and excited fit to burst on account of the sheer naturalness with which she said this, like she'd expected nothing less from me, and I'm glad I did that little thing which caused her to be charmed by me. I want to charm her some more, that's for sure, so I get to thinking how I can go about it, humming along to myself as I get busy prising open the oysters.

The light is all but gone now so, mindful of the mosquitoes, I check that the door and windows are shut tight and flick on the light, which makes the pool glow, looking pretty beneath the trees. As I'm standing by the door contemplating this fact I hear music, almost celestial-sounding as it is carried towards me on the evening air. I turn round and from this angle I can just see her back, sideways on, as she's setting up the stereo player, turning the volume up some more, looking through my music collection carefully, pulling out records, putting them on top of the machine. I stand dead still, liking to watch her do this ordinary thing in my house, unable to help myself wondering if there could ever be a time when I'd not feel the tenderness I feel towards her now as she does this little thing, just choosing music on a quiet Saturday evening alone together at home. But then it's like she feels my eyes on her and she turns. The light is low inside, so I can't see the precise expression on her face and guess she can't see mine either, so I raise a hand to let her know I can see her and she does the same thing, mirroring me, neither of us speaking. Then it's as if she's drawn on a string, reeled in towards me, just where I want her to be, as though my wanting it had the power to make it actually happen, so that now she's beside me and we're both watching the still surface of the pool gleam in the night beneath the trees. We don't touch but we're standing close enough for me to feel the heat burning out from her body towards me.

Suddenly, there's a banging, clumsy crashing sound from inside the house and we look at one another, I swear it's the look of disappointed conspirators, but still, conspirators! I think, as we listen to the Swissman coming back after his nap. I get to the kitchen on the double, so there's no need for explanation, not that there was anything to explain. She takes her time, standing by the back door, probably watching the mosquitoes flashing around through the darkness, their little wings catching glimpses of the light from the pool.

'Sorry, I was sleeping,' the Swissman says.

'Don't be sorry,' I reply to him, rather too hasty and sincere.

He goes across to the sofa, picking up the bottle of whisky, trailing it after him limply like he's had enough already, but who am I to complain? and sits down heavily among the heaped-up cushions. 'I'm not very hungry. You two must eat without me,' he says thickly so I can tell he's really gone, then falls asleep almost straight away before he's finished speaking.

The girl comes back into the kitchen, singing along softly to the music, John Coltrane, that she'd put on the machine earlier, looking happy and relaxed, and in my opinion more beautiful by the second. She comes through to where I'm standing looking at the Swissman asleep on the sofa, trying to figure out a way to get rid of him. Before she realises he's still here, she laughs, saying, 'Hey, you're shirking your duties in the kitchen, come on.' Then seeing him, she puts a hand to her mouth as though to stop more words coming out and quickly looks at me with an obvious thought in her mind, exactly the same disappointment and frustration as mine: *What are we going to do?* The decision is taken before I can help myself. 'C'mon, can you give me a hand, he needs his bed I reckon,' which makes her grin and grin like a Cheshire cat and I feel like a kid on a first date who suddenly realises how to undo a girl's bra and get to those delicious, strange parts he's heard so much about, those things he's felt as a child and always longed to return to. So we get to heaving and dragging, panting with the effort of lifting him – and he's not light, I assure you. I take hold of him under his armpits and she starts off lifting his long, dangling legs, but he's too heavy for her and I can manage him by myself now anyway, so I drag him along without much problem down the back hallway to his room on the far side of the house, with her dancing around silently alongside and in front of me. We get him into the bedroom, where she takes hold of his ankles again to heave him on to the bed, and we leave him spread-eagled, out cold, snoring deeply the moment he's there like it's the middle of the night. We stand for a moment, looking down at his prone shape, her putting a hand against her mouth like she's just about to burst out belly-laughing. Then I take her other hand, which seems like the right thing to do in the darkness of that room with him already snoring like a skinny hog, and I lead her out of there and back through to the kitchen to go get us some dinner.

There is a gold-embossed sign fixed on to the door to the library: 'Quiet please, people are working' and I always find it encouraging to be so nonchalantly embraced within this category of people with legitimate purpose. Especially on days like today when the words leap dangerously even as I set them down, jostling into one another like a feisty crowd, brewing agitation. There are few people in here now, when the evening is stretching out across the city and the crowding cars race home through the drowning neon. What people there are remain unseen and sink surreptitiously into the gloomy corners of the vast room, snuffling quietly to themselves, seldom looking up from their reading. Eyes hardly ever meet in here. It is a good place to write. I have worked here for many years. I find that it helps to have a simulation of order when the odd black marks upon the page become inscrutable, threatening to make a life of their own and lead me on into it with unflinching disinterest, enjoying their neat revelations.

Furtive people are the ones most often found in this library. People who need their secret time alone in order to live with some degree of propriety in their other lives, the ones they return to at the end of each day's work. Where would they be without their secret time? Slipping down the rain-washed pavements in a street somewhere far from home, dreaming of hands around the stranger's throat, the cold cut of the knife's elegant damage; silently waiting, stretched out on their backs beneath a favourite tree in the park, watching the swinging clouds overhead; numbing the tumble of lunacy with drink, never enough to stop up the mouth which mutters *more* and then shouts unhappily about how much it has forgotten; striding the world like a madman, yearning to feel the pull back home but never feeling it, driven instead by the wild delight of strange places like a memory drug which says: your home is everywhere where you are undiluted by attachments, so you are not looking but merely finding and re-finding, the world become a mirror to remind yourself of your own lifelong monsters which squat inside your mind, chewing up and tearing out all your thoughts, deliberately and without remorse.

It is late. Beyond the high windows the night begins again. There is half an hour before closing time. I've finished what I meant to do today but am loath to leave, preferring to inhale the musty paperish soup in here than the sharp November air outside in the streets. I can see no one. I get up and shuffle across to the book stacks, idling along them until I come to the section where my own name stares back at me. Twenty-seven volumes, the stories of my life, tidied up and neatly gagged, silently suffocating in clear plastic covers. That's all my life amounts to: twenty-seven murder attempts. He lurks in each one of these books, sometimes disguised as the charming friend with a sinister secret passion, or the buffoon, pitiful and easy to mock. Sometimes he's the obvious villain, despised throughout the entire story and redeemed in the final pages as the victim of chance, her one true love, a suitable hero. At other times he is affectionately hidden within a phrase or a gesture. Often it's just a matter of syntax and I steal his phrasing like a backhanded compliment, trying to imagine how it was for him. I often come here when no one is looking. Picking up the different books is a reassurance that I exist. Here's the proof of it. Things have gone on. Time has passed. I have happened. I smile to myself, feeling the futility of it all like a gently whipping wind, licking me damply until I shiver with it, saddened and amused.

I wander further along the silent rows until I come to the section where he is, two whole shelves of him, stacked up around lip height. I touch the spines of the books one by one, briefly, following the curves of his name with my fingertips as though it were magic Braille and by touching the letters I could spirit him into the present. And it's true. If I shut my eyes tight enough I can feel his breath upon the back of my neck and his hands running the length of my frail spine as though he had messages to write upon my skin, secret sentences intended to live and die with me. But it doesn't work this way: as I turn the pages I see only the streams of persistent codes lingering after him, lying in wait for the endless years of word-hungry people to find them, decipher them and forget them, making room for more.

I take one of his books out at random and walk with it pressed tightly under my arm back to the place where my books are, slipping it in between two blue-backed volumes so that our names run in parallel, close up against one another, touching but not joining, a little act of absurd sabotage which gives me great pleasure.

~

The light from the heavy evening sun is all but gone as we walk together through the silent house and it seems only natural that I should set about lighting a fire. I reflect that this is the first time I've done that for quite a few years but it looks pretty and makes our evening together feel like it's beginning, now that we're alone, with the darkness outside gathering us up in its soft embrace. A sense of exquisite ease and anticipation settles over me, filling my heart up with joy. Pure joy is what it is. It's a feeling brimful with newness, every other moment of happiness throughout my life just falling away, absolutely irrelevant to this sensation. All I can think is: *I wouldn't change a single thing*.

There are no lights on anywhere in the house, so the only illumination comes from the fire now burning brightly in the hearth, the pale pine logs giving off an aroma of fresh earth and mountain-sides. As it grows darker outside, the intensity of the flames appears to grow ever more jewel-like. I stand for a moment to contemplate and memorise everything before going through to the kitchen. She is barefoot and is leaning towards the window, stretched forward on her toes, still wearing the apron, so I surprise her by coming up behind her and undoing the ties at the back, saying, 'Let's eat, honey.' And as she stands back down, my hand rests against her back briefly and the inevitability of having further chances to get close to her is so sweet. We carry the food through to the other room and sit beside one another at one end of the table and I feel like a king.

Salty water runs down her chin while she eats the oysters. I can hardly bear to look. When she sees me staring I lean towards her and wipe the juice away with a corner of my napkin. She touches her lips where the cloth passed over her skin and looks at me with such unmistakable desire I straight away think I must've imagined it.

She has a big appetite, just like I knew she would, and I love to see that quality in a woman, especially one glowing with health and life as she is. We get to work on the crab-claws next and by now, I should mention, we've just come to the end of our first bottle of wine so I go get the next one, saying, 'This is really pleasant, isn't this pleasant?' feeling like I ought to use a word like that otherwise I'll just get down on all fours and start baying like a hound I'm so hot for her. I come swinging back over to the table, thinking *This is life, this is how to do it!* At last, after all these years, I've realised how to do it. Somewhere in my mind I'm on the brink of accepting defeat, thinking that if it goes no further than this, if on the surface it's only dinner, then I won't mind because it's *such* a dinner, but at the same time I'm overflowing with all the promises I glimpsed in that look she just gave me back then when I cleaned her face up and I know, I just know, there's a chance and I've got to fight for it.

So I get busy, cracking open crab-claws for her, both of us aware that she's perfectly capable of doing this little thing herself, but there being something exciting just in the process of me tussling over the reddened shell while she waits for me to pass her the broken-up claws and hums along to the jazz we've got playing. We carry on like that, me cracking, wrestling, handing her the pure white flesh, sometimes forking dollops of it on to her plate or handing her the full fork so she can eat it that way, me then surreptitiously licking the fork as I eat my mouthful of it, smiling to myself that she doesn't know this little trick I'm playing on her.

And then we're done. The debris of dinner is scattered across the table any old how, heaped up in front of us like we're two peasants at a feast. We both lean back in our chairs, smiling at one another, talking about simple things that are of course the only things that count at a moment like this: the sound of the dark trees rustling beyond the windows, the crackling fire, the fact that John Coltrane is indisputably a genius, how those crab-claws were the finest in all the world, what a wonderful day we've had. Of course, there's no mention of any time beyond the seconds we're having right now.

Looking at me with a sudden mischievous grin, she reaches over and pinches me lightly on the bare skin of my arm with a crab-claw. I yelp out loud in an exaggerated fashion as though it hurt, picking up another claw and snapping its little pincers shut like I'm going to pinch her too and we both laugh and laugh at this as we take the stuff off the table and through into the dark kitchen, where both of us are reluctant to turn on the light. It seems so much more appropriate for us to be stumbling around together in the gloom, with just the occasional flickering from off of the fire in the other room.

Minute by minute I am getting an ever stronger feeling of being in unison with her, like we're having exactly the same thoughts about each other. It suddenly strikes me that way and it's like we're playing, or doing some wonderful elaborate dance always edging into the inevitable pleasure, the final moves. It's never been like that for me with women.

I've always been dogged by a sensation of one of us leading, you know, either me *trying it on*, as women call it, which is a kind of humiliation I've always thought, or else me fending them off, or trying to keep them happy in some way without letting on that my heart simply isn't in it. So this evening the whole thing comes as a shock to me, realising that it's possible for two people to be together in this way of equal excitement, equal anticipation.

'Let's leave the rest,' I say, gesturing towards the mess of our feast. Then she stops for a moment in front of me, wiping her hands on a cloth, standing just a foot or so away. I can see her smiling at me in the darkness, her red hair gleaming around her head, and I want to take hold of her and lead her upstairs, make love to her right now, but instead I say, 'Brandy?' and we both laugh like we're sharing in the joke of our mutual drunkenness. The moment has gone but still lingers between us: I know she felt it too. 'Brandy' of course also means 'the other room sitting by the fireside' which is where we go now, both of us knocking into things in the unsteady light thrown around the room by the leaping flames.

I fuss around with the glasses, uncork a new bottle of cognac while she pulls some cushions off the sofa and lies down on them in front of the fire, propping herself up on one elbow, suddenly seeming lost in herself as she looks at the quiet fire roaring away in front of her. And while I watch her lying there like that I try to imagine anything more perfect than this, than her, and I can't do it. I pull out a cushion and sit beside her, handing her a glass of brandy which she takes, avoiding looking me in the eyes, just taking the glass with a tiny smile that makes her seem, briefly, lost, so I ask her, 'You OK?'

She turns to me and says in a voice at once casual and right from her heart so I know she means it, 'I've never been happier.' She looks in my eyes with a question for a brief moment and starts to turn back to the fire again, but I reach over to her and touch her hair, which makes her jump slightly, and then she's turning back to me saying, 'Please, I want to kiss you,' and we move towards one another like two natural magnets. We're drawn together fast but so sweetly, like the end of a race, almost exhausted with it, and I kiss her lips for the first time, tasting the salty oysters on her hot breath, wrapping my hands up in her burning hair, both of us pulling each other towards ourselves as though to get back what is by rights our own. We tip and slide over, falling towards each other, deeply into each other's arms like twins tumbling in play and she clings to me, drawing me

153

closer to get the whole length of my body against her, and I'm surprised and excited by her strength and the strength of her desire for me, old man that I am, beyond hope yet suddenly given this chance of life which God knows I don't deserve. But for now I'm not thinking about anything but how sweet this feels and how much sweeter it would be if only we were naked and I were inside her, so I start getting fixed on that one idea and it's like she's having the same thoughts precisely, down to the last detail because she groans deeply and kneels up, pulling me with her, 'Come on, please, we have to – ' she says and I can't believe my luck that this lovely creature wants me. Whatever she wants to do to me, she can have me all, not that I'm much, but what it is, it's all hers.

We stagger to our feet, both of us clinging to one another as though we're drowning in the flickering waves from off the fire, lighting up our bodies strangely. We stand swaying together for a moment and for some reason can't start our feet in motion, so give up trying and just sink back down to the floor again, each weighing down the other, and I'm sinking beneath the completeness of my feeling for her, becoming almost short of breath, gasping with wanting her, overwhelmed by the sheer joy of the situation, here like this with her. We're kneeling together now, supporting one another but also dragging the other underneath the surface of our lust to see what goes on there, then my mouth is upon her neck, drawing out the taste of her skin, and she's lifting my shirt off over my head, become cat-like in the way she licks at my flesh like she wants to eat it, her rough little tongue running up and down my chest while I bury my hands deeper into the curve of her waist, drawing her hips towards me, feeling the shape of her, pressing her tight up against me, realising with surprise and pride that I am as hard as a horny teenager, something I want her to discover at the earliest possible moment, which she seems to understand as she takes my cock in her hands briefly before slipping her mouth over me and sucking me like she can't get enough, so I'm on the point of losing it entirely the very second her lips touch my skin.

I pull her head back, thinking *I don't believe I just stopped her from doing that, am I mad*? But her mouth's sweet taste is reward enough for this restraint, then her breasts there in front of me when I open the downwards-travelling buttons along the front of her pale-green dress, the same buttons I've been longing to undo all damn day and here I am doing just that, taking one of her breasts in my mouth, making her moan and claw at my back like a wild thing before I gently topple her over backwards so I can get my whole body up against hers, feeling her legs opening to let me inside, and inside I go, crazily entering her like it's my first time, her pulling me into her like I'm trying to get away is how it seems, when my only thought is how to get further into her, as far as I can go, searching out that point where our pleasures lie, wrapped up together, waiting to be disturbed and shaken from sleep, nudged into wakefulness, now burning meteor-bright as I'm bursting into her, and she makes a noise that's half howl, half sob – or maybe that was me – but certainly it's her legs tight around my back, one arm raised above her head, holding herself steady against the wall, the other hauling me into her, heaving against my back. But now her hands have gone suddenly limp, twining into my hair, and I just manage to muster the strength to look up at her face which is gleaming like a visionary, bright-shining and full of wonder and ecstatic sadness. I expect this is exactly the way my face must be looking from the way she smiles at me with tenderness and something else in her eyes like she's just been made aware for the first time of how abandoned people can get at moments like this – if they're lucky enough ever to find moments like this at any stage throughout their long, lonely lives, like I almost didn't, which is God's honest truth. I almost didn't ever get this lucky. A whole world was there within me and I hadn't suspected a thing. It's just mind-numbing how blind a person can be.

I am the last to leave the library tonight, so, apart from the librarian, the place is empty. As I go, gathering up my things, I watch her broguishly plodding the bookstacks and try to imagine what she does in here after everyone has left: how long she stays, whether she thinks of this place as her own, if she hates the people who come here to study while she catalogues and lists, keeping things in order. She never meets my eye, nor does she ever speak, even when there is no one else here, apart from her triumphant 'Closing up, please' clarion call each evening.

Outside, the night is sharp with the chance of frost. People stamp by, thumping the pavements to heat their feet, dreaming of home and food, eager to get inside somewhere, anywhere that is out of the cold. There are no clouds tonight and the half-full moon glides among the bright stars, unveiled and surprising above the tiny street lights. I set off through the fast flood of people. There are baying paper-sellers on the street corners and a man offering roast chestnuts outside the tube station, clamping his naked fingers against the warm metal barrel to find heat.

As I walk, the tide of people ebbs and flows about me, sometimes clustering up around the roadside, then thinning out along a back street, alternately crowding and dispersing in one vast stream of turbulent footsteps, dawdling and determined. Never a moment passes when I'm not scanning the crowds of strange faces to see if one of them is his. The precision of loneliness is unflinching. It cuts to the heart to scrape out the exact quantity of meat: always just enough to destroy a person, never enough to erase them from memory.

Many of the people in the crowd are familiar, though unknown. Their moonish faces loom and dissolve around me, reminders of all the attempts I've made to slough him off my skin from where he won't budge, stuck fast like a saturating tattoo, inking me right through from front to back, painting me a different colour from my guts to the tips of my finger-nails. Tonight, as I look again at all these faces, I remember the fast and lingering liaisons which have clung about me like diseases over the long years of my life, dangling from about my neck, infecting me with themselves, none of them able to shift the quiet stink of the illness he gave me: himself.

How I've tried to rid myself of him. The dark back streets, the risky bedsit tusslings in God knows where, the church-blessed unions, the delirious tryings-on of countless new lives to see if there's one which will fit well enough to leave no space for him, all of this in vain. So now when I press on against the unrelenting current of strangers I feel men and women surging through me like an army of the dead. Every one of them transformed into a story, each sucked dry by my vampire's glare of despondency as I see their loveliness fall from them like rotten flesh to join my own, scattered in pieces along the bed of our messy desires. And all I'm left with is the echo of tenacious bones, clattering on against the up-filling pages which are littered with the carcasses of lovers and friends finally become no more than haggard, strange shapes upon a page, all of them now merely words, myself included, the only persistent, undead thing: him.

However calmly I walk and however tightly I screw up my mind to avoid them, still the words, the wraiths of these lost people, clutter like lice around me, so that I have to walk faster to try to shake them off, madly scratching my flesh to dislodge them, gouging them out from the roots of my hair where they burrow and lay eggs which hatch and multiply when I am inattentive. By then it is too late and I'm already overrun.

I look downwards at the pavement, not wanting people to see the look of horror and revulsion swilling around in my eyes and twisting down the edges of my mouth in an ugly scowl, making me look like a death's head. But nobody looks at me any more. It happened gradually. When I was young it was difficult to go anywhere without eyes upon me, their sneaking looks spawning paranoia: *What are they thinking? Why do they say these things to me?* But now that I'm old I can creep around unobtrusively. People leave me alone. I prefer it like this. It makes it so much easier to watch them.

As I near home, a wind picks up across the city, drawing out the breath from the streets so that people close their mouths tight shut, as though fearing that their souls will be sucked from them and scattered across the streets like ashes, lost for ever among the swaying building tops and the gaps between the stars glinting hotly overhead, oblivious.

~

I wake up in pain. A thin light fingers open my eyelids, wresting me roughly from sleep. She isn't here. I'm alone, as ever, in my bed, the sheets wound uncomfortably around my body. I feel as though I've barely slept and what sleep I had was fitful, disturbed and against my will. Today, this morning, is the day she leaves and, anyway, she's not here at this moment which grips me with horror. *She isn't here.* I turn over and smell her sweet skin on my own, my entire body feeling bruised and sore as though I've been beaten up. Her imprint is upon me now, raw and for ever. I hate the dawn which marks the day she leaves.

Of course, her being married and my imminent death doesn't have to mean the end, but it does, it simplifies the end. At least, that's what I try to tell myself. The end! Look at me, there was barely a beginning. What am I thinking? And am I forgetting the fact that if I were lucky enough to reach eighty, a mere five years from now, she'd be just turning twenty-five. The figures speak for themselves. And anyway, if my goddamn doctor is to

162

be believed I won't even see the year out. So what am I? Some kind of monster who wants deliberately to inflict my death-pangs upon this lovely young thing? Even if by some miracle it were possible to keep my worn-out heart ticking for ten more years it would still mean she'd probably have half a century more of living without me, fifty years of being a widow. How could I do that to her? Love won't let me do that to her. And now I've said it. For the first time, I've said it, knowing that at last I mean it, that in the shadowy final years of my sorry life I've been touched by love and was powerless to prevent it from the first moment I set eyes on her. *What can I do?* is all I can think, that solitary howl the only thing in my conscious mind, the rest of me still filled up with endless visions, images and fantasies about what we did and could still do together, had things been any way but as they in fact are.

I heave my old rebelling limbs up and over the edge of the bed, gripping my head between my hands so it doesn't explode, covering my eyes with my fists, unable to stop the hot tears from falling, endlessly falling, filling my hands with a salt wetness that can only remind me of her. All things lead to her. Good and bad, even indifferent, they all direct my soul towards her whether I like it or not.

Somehow I get from the edge of the bed to the shower and seeing my body in the mirror reminds me of a time, only yesterday, when I'd looked at it and felt reassured, thinking that the mere age of it meant that there was no danger or possibility of anything happening between us. I look at it now and can see only the body that she desires. It doesn't belong to me any more. My body has been remade entirely by her lust and I stare hard, trying to fathom what it might be that she wants from it, raising up each arm in turn, looking at the limply dying muscles, even the skin turning grey like unused parchment left to rot in a forgotten attic. The more I stare the more I feel the weight of impossibility and the creeping return of security. This burgeoning sense of hopelessness is strange comfort, but it's all I have and so I cling to it.

Feeling unfamiliar to myself, I dress carefully, trying not to disturb the echo of her body against mine which I want to sustain for as long as I can, keep it safe against my skin so that I can listen to it when she's gone. 'When she's gone.' I say these words out loud, watching them shape my mouth into the O of a kiss, listening to the solemn sound of this simple fact, only a very little fact in the end, someone's not being here not actually meaning anything in itself, not really being final – but it is, of course, so I go downstairs like I'm going to my execution. Her bags are already packed and waiting beside the front door, and I nearly give up right then and just sit down on the stairs and weep. Instead, deep-breathing, I go out into the garden for a while, staring up at the vacant sky, trying to make myself at least appear calm, thinking I might as well just walk away from here, just walk until I fall down dead because what makes any more sense than that? But I don't do this for the simple reason that by the time I turn back towards the house I see her, standing in the kitchen with her back to me, talking to the Swissman. And all it takes is the merest sight of her to send my heart soaring, make me forget everything but the blind happiness I feel at the simple fact of her existence.

I'm acutely aware of how difficult I could make things for her, which is the last thing I want. I'm not a shit, however hard I've tried over the years.

She turns round and her face breaks into a broad calm-seeming smile when she sees me. My heart is breaking in two, so there's another expression I've only just understood, I remark to myself, except *breaking* isn't the word I'd use. I'd be looking for a word more like stabbed, or maybe hammered, smashed, wrenched, ripped, stamped, kicked, sliced with a blunt knife, the expression would have to be something more like that if I'd been the one making it up and, even then, I'd have been

165

disappointed in the mismatching of such words to the sensation of extraordinary anguish that I'm feeling as I look at her now. I start assuming I'm just about to fall down dead and have the wild impression that perhaps I'm just having a coronary and it's not love at all, which is a ludicrous enough thought to get me through the next ten minutes while the Swissman is loitering around so there's no chance for us to speak even a single word (what is there to say? I'd need a lifetime, which is precisely the thing we don't have).

She gathers her things together and then there they both are sitting side by side in the car like today is just an ordinary day, one like any other, and the car is pulling out of the driveway with her in it. She's smiling at me in a way I can't fathom and sneezing is how it looks, which seems crazier still but gives me the chance to give her the neckerchief I'm wearing that day, saying, 'Keep it, please.' For some reason it gives me some comfort to think that she has something tangible of mine, even if it is a stupid red spotted neckerchief, but when I give it to her our fingers touch briefly and I actually jump backwards with the jolt of pain and memory I get at her touch and she looks at me in that same way she looked at me last night when I pounded my life out into her, giving her every last thing I have. That paltry neckerchief becomes in my mind a pathetic coda to whatever it was that passed between us this brief weekend and I stare at it, rather than at her, feeling resentful but glad that at least some part of me is with her until such time as she loses it, throws it away or gives it to someone else. Oh, my life, I can barely find breath or expression for this, so I'm merely backing away, waving I think, as the car pulls out of the driveway, and I walk a few paces towards the empty space, saying wildly into the empty air, 'Why not stay? Can't you stay for a little while longer?' then sobbing, actually sobbing like a madman, into the emptiness which only a few seconds ago was filled with her.

Throughout the night the wind rattles the broken tree-tops and whips up the uncut grass until it lies flat against the hard earth. Around four, unable to sleep, I put on a thick coat and go outside. Beyond the line of bending poplars at the bottom of the garden the river shimmers weirdly in the moon-light, ripped up across the gnarled surface by strange fingers of wind and mysterious eddies creeping upwards from the river bed. The twisting silver skin belies its depth, making it seem puddle-shallow and full of light, with moonbeams heaped up along the curved dish of limpid water, grating softly against one another to make their brightness dance upwards, touching the surface. But the flood runs deep, even at the height of summer, when it sinks well below the murky waterline and carries with it the slow weight of mud from upriver.

I watch the water, sitting on a wooden bench on the brink of it, beneath the softly shuffling trees. The wind freezes my gloveless hands until they are useless and I sink deeper within my heavy coat wondering when the year suddenly became so cold. On nights like this the only sounds are the infrequent calls of the birds skimming the river a few inches above the surface and the creaking of the naked branches of the trees, shaken by the strong wind. From the far side the lights from the warehouses shed a sallow, constant glow towards me so that I am drenched in pale, artificial light. Sitting here this quietly, I feel as though I could become a part of the land, just collapse into the silent river along with the drenched grass, sagging into the water all along the banks beside me.

A tremendous calm keeps me out here long after the cold wind has cut through to my fragile bones and turned my old blood sluggish with effort, making me tremble with it. I remember certain things and I let myself drift, suspended for a few minutes above the fast surface of my life.

He told me how he loved to sit beside the sea alone and especially in the darkness, letting the slow heave of the Atlantic lift and lower him, imagining he was a thing without past or future, merely persisting through the present moment without burden or purpose. And perhaps the magnetic flood of the tides did loosen his life from him, momentarily. Only now, beside the river, I feel the weight of time sweeping through me and bearing me along with it, the whole panoply of events weighing heavily around my shoulders, giving me

169

no release at all, the bleak ecstasy I'm feeling now not coming from any illusion of loss but from the shock of the brute facts of my life hanging about my neck and not lost for ever as I'd like them to be. I am suddenly like a lead brain hurtling earthwards, everything sensation and thought, unable to slow the downward dive. The intense regret I feel at all the missed chances in my life is overwhelming. I shudder at the waste of it all. I long for it to be drawn away from me and to seep off into the river so that I can at last be free. I try to forget.

I turn my back on the river and go up to the empty house, wading upwards against the flow of the thick grass on the steeply sloping lawn which glows, shivering like the sea beneath moonlight. My fourth husband died last year and now I live alone. There is one light on in the house, upstairs in the bedroom.

I smile to myself to think how perfectly my life has mirrored his. There's solace in this symmetry. Running in parallel, though separated by a lifetime, the similarities of our two old lives add up to something, I often tell myself. It's as though, by my deliberate imitation, I have plucked us both out of time and welded our lives tightly together in some other world, far away from here but infinitely more real, unthwarted by the limpet facts that

170

blighted us both, ruining everything. That one short time when we overlapped sent ripples out across both of our lives, forwards and backwards in time, vibrating through everything that happened before or since we met like a rock dropped from a great height, die-straight to the bottom of the river.

That it couldn't, *shouldn't* even, be possible to make a whole life out of a weekend is now of no consequence. It has happened. I could do nothing about it. I have loved him and lived with him in the greatest part of myself throughout my life, the secret part of myself where I really live. *And here's the proof.* I smile to myself as I pass the rows of books in the hallway, stamping my feet against the floor to get some heat back into the frail bones.

Walking past the tall mirror in the hallway I catch sight of my reflection. Fragile and shrunken, my skull seems to be too heavy for my body which is bent over, concave, as though suddenly winded, with all the breath pushed out of it. My feet seem huge and hideously comical in their big brown men's shoes, stuck oddly on to the end of two stiff bones, once legs, now no more than sticks to lift around with me, little better than walking canes and less resilient. Inside this huge coat I look like a grotesquely wrinkled child, caught dressing up and wearing a clown's wig of bright white candyfloss hair, tied up with a girlish ribbon into a dishevelled knot at the back of my nodding head. At what point did I stop recognising myself? I forget. And when I lift my hand up to push aside a strand of hair from my eyes, the claw-like fingers appal me, my right hand bent into the perfect shape for writing, curled round upon itself, barely needing to grip any more to hold a pen, so bent in upon itself is it.

Sometimes, catching myself off guard like this, to lessen the shock I try to imagine him standing behind me in the mirror, his hand upon my tiny shoulder, his broad face smiling at me from out of the glass, both of us hating our age and discontented as hell, but determined, too, and full of tenderness for one another, above all, full of tenderness.

~

Mornings are the worst. It's then that things happen. I'm not being specific. Just stuff starting to happen again, with me not able to do a solitary thing about it. Suicide is too good for me. I don't deserve to be released from this anguish which is a kind of salvation in a way, is what I tell myself. And whoever said salvation was supposed to be an easy ride?

So there's sunshine, people on the phone to me yak yak yakking about whatever, there are chores to do around the house, birthdays, Christmas on the way, children playing somewhere I shouldn't doubt it, and generally stuff happening regardless of the fact she's gone. She's gone! I say it out loud sometimes, laughing my head off. I even turn it into little songs, 'She's gone, la la, she's gone, tiddlypom, oh yeah, she's gone gone gone yaaadiya!' Some days I even do a merry jig to see how that feels and it feels fine, my ancient legs wincing at the strain of elevation and fall, just like they should, so sometimes when they hurt only a little bit I give them an extra hard *stamp* as I come back down to the ground, so they really hurt and bam! I feel instantly better, this being the proper order of things, the kind of state I should be in.

Now I understand things a little better. Whisperings in the street when I go into the town for supplies to sustain my isolation: 'There's that weird hermit I told you about, Madge darling. Just look at him!' And I think *Yes! C'mon, stare some more, what the hell's stopping you throwing stones at me? I'd like that. That's how it should be, get on with it you miserable bastards, show me something I can really get a laugh out of.* But they never do. Rotten swine, can't even find the heart to do that much for me.

'Oh yes!' I sing as I stroll around my garden, swigging from a bottle of whisky, looking up at the pretty sun and the lovely blue sky without a single cloud to spoil it. 'She's gone and she's not coming back, never, never, never.' Of course, for me, *never* is such a short time. When you think of the years when she wasn't here, the fact that she isn't going to come again is nothing compared with that immense desert of barren, blind anticipation, so blind it didn't even realise that that's what it was. Now *there's* something to get sorry over, which is what I do most days.

So now I'm strolling round my garden, prodding the plants, throwing stones at the birds, sticks at the stray cats and lumps of whatever I can lay my hands on just wherever, just chucking stuff around. It's kind of fun after a while and I've spent the morning writing, so I feel that I can take the day off if I want to and I don't feel strongly about it either way, so I do it just to pass the time which is now something I have even less of. So there's another thing she messed up, I reflect to myself. I'd started to become almost happy with the thought that soon I wouldn't ever be able to pick up a pen again in my life. But the witch set me off writing and rewriting in earnest, digging up old neglected books, polishing them up and sending them out into the world, fixing me back on that miserable, demented search, that pointless staring at myself, that stupid chattering about all the ways I've wasted my life, that dim, feverish remembering of things not worth dredging up they're so pointless. The bottle's empty now so I hurl it at the pool house and it clangs off the wooden veranda, not even breaking, which amuses me no end.

I go off down to the vegetable plot, sauntering through the long, pleasant summer afternoon to check on my greenhouse, to take a look and see if the kids have thrown any more stones. But no, the nasty brats are getting more well-behaved by the day, which seriously infuriates me, what's wrong with them? *Since she's been gone*, I think, they've been much better behaved. Really, it was around the time she went that they started acting all well-mannered, never doing a thing wrong, whereas *before she came* they were always doing what bad kids should, wreaking havoc in my garden at even the slightest opportunity. Maybe it's because they spotted me one day doing a wild, happy dance beside the wrecked potato plants, fairly whooping with delight at the way they'd messed them up. Now *that* was a day. Everything went wrong. At last things felt like I reckon they should do. It even rained! I remember going outside to jump around for joy in the storm that night, just waiting to be struck by lightning but the bastard upstairs wasn't playing dice.

So here I still am, watching over my tomato plants which look as though they're up for some kind of poxy prize all of their own accord since they are flourishing like there's no tomorrow. They simply won't die, despite my best efforts to the contrary. I swear that girl put a hex on them just like she did on me. I've put poison on the bastards, I've stamped on them, even poured boiling water on their roots, done all manner of unspeakable things to them, but take a look! They won't give up. This is all her fault, for a fact. It's a sorry state of affairs when even a man's tomato plants aren't sympathetic to his situation I can tell you.

It's always the same, so what am I going to do about it?

Contemplating this question, I carry on with the day, as the sun stretches itself out across the brightly uninterrupted blue above me, gradually fading into a night like any other. It's all I can do.

I flick the lights on, one by one, on my way upstairs, hating the darkness. In the bedroom, I stretch out flat on my back on the bed beneath the tight covers and wait for morning. Tomorrow, I have people coming to stay for the weekend: my publisher and her young friend, another writer. It will be nice to have people around in the house which has started to feel terribly empty now that there is only me in it.

There seems to be less and less light recently, the days gradually shortening as the year grows old, edging towards midwinter. Autumn used to be my favourite time of year. The smell of the settling earth meant new college terms and hurried resolutions, expectations and energies running high as I raced to finish things. But now I have so little fire left in me. Thoughts of new beginnings make me faint-hearted. Every day becomes hard. I decay unassailably. I grow suspicious of illness and fearful of sleep, wondering about my dreams of emptiness and vast, unpeopled spaces.

But I am tired, more tired than I ever remember feeling before, as though I have just run a race and can't bring my limbs to lift any further than where they are now, flat out and exhausted. I drift in and out of wakefulness, only my mind refusing to rest, tearing forwards and backwards across random thoughts, vague plans for new books, irrelevant details about things I must do before the people arrive tomorrow, friends I ought to telephone next week, the gorgeous shape of the moon shining through the window, patterning the bedcovers with its watery light.

Of course, I also think about him. Just idle, comforting thoughts as a small child might dream of milk, floating sweetly through my mind as I drift towards sleep. I see his face watching me with the same curious alertness with which he looked at me that first evening when I arrived at his house, just as the day darkened into night and we three went inside together, laughing and talking about the state of the world, planning the weekend ahead of us. And as often happens when I sail the moon into sleep, I see him vividly beside me and can feel his caresses lighting up my skin, moving hotly over my ancient body throughout the night.

Now we're lying together on the bed, watching the heavy moon start its slow sink into dawn, the mild evaporation of darkness something wonderful to see as the sun rises, inching up towards the horizon. With his body wrapped right around me and mine around his there's nothing between us apart from a thin skin of heat. Our breathing matches. It is the only sound in the empty room. Morning is still some hours away and we have not slept, made light and nerve-tight with lack of rest.

I turn round to face him, tracing along the line of his brows and the ridge of his nose with my wanton fingertips, feeling the familiar shapes, noticing the changing textures of his skin, loosening with age like my own. He opens his eyes and kisses me softly, then with passion, and we cling together, tussling like wild animals in the last moments of moonlight, grinning foolishly at one another as though we have no idea how the story will go: the push towards pleasure, the ringing out of every last drop of delight, until we both collapse, sated and happy like fat things in the sun.

But now, when I turn over, caught on the downward swing into sleep, I see him standing a little distance away from me, looking at me with an odd smile upon his lips: the smile of a complete stranger. I watch, incredulous. I wait. 'You'll forget about me soon enough,' he says softly, still smiling that unfamiliar, sad smile. He turns away from me, then looks back briefly, just once, before walking away and out of the room, closing the door quietly as he leaves. I watch him go, feeling the whole long stream of years rushing out from me, a violent haemorrhaging of events which have driven me and my dying body on through life until the end which is *now*, many years too late but still far sooner than I'd ever imagined possible. And all there's left in me is the geography of my love for him. As though the map of years, like a burning blindfold, has been pressed across my eyes, setting fire to everything. Now I'm so used to the burn I don't know how to live without it, don't want to live without it, but can't bear to open my eyes to the darkness, raging against the failing light which is ebbing faster and faster from me, a horrible final tide which I'm not ready for and don't want to face alone. But he's gone and will never return to me, not even beyond this oozing death which is covering over my eyes as all the dearest events of my life, those moments with him, rush past me in one last out-breath of wild, hot sorrow until I feel the disease spitting out my ragged flesh and lifting away from me like a final caress.

My body trembles. I sweat with the effort of living. I ache. I watch the closed door and know that it will never open again, that he has looked at me for the last time.

~

Also available in Vintage

Ian McEwan

ENDURING LOVE

'I cannot remember the last time I read a novel so beautifully
written or utterly compelling from the very first page'
Bill Bryson, *Sunday Times*

'A page-turner, with a plot so engrossing that it seems reckless to pick the book up in the evening if you plan to get any
sleep that night...*Enduring Love* is also blessed with the
psychological richness of the finest literary novel'
Alain de Botton, *Daily Mail*

'Taut with narrative excitements and suspense...a novel of
rich diversity that triumphantly integrates imagination and
intelligence, rationality and emotional alertness'
Peter Kemp, *Sunday Times*

'He is the maestro at creating suspense: the particular, sick-
ening, see-sawing kind that demands a kind of physical
courage from the reader to continue reading'
Amanda Craig, *New Statesman*

'McEwan's exploration of his characters' lives and secret
emotions is a virtuoso display of fictional subtlety and
intelligence'
Robert McCrum, *Observer*

VINTAGE